WILL BE

DEMONS

THE REALM SERIES

AE JONES

AE Jones: Demons Will Be Demons
Copyright © 2018 by Amy E Jones

Publisher: Gabby Reads Publishing LLC

Cover Designer: http://theillustratedauthor.net/
Editor: http://www.demonfordetails.com/
Formatter: http://www.authorems.com/

ISBN-13: 978-1-941871-20-1

ACKNOWLEDGMENTS

To Melissa, thanks for creating brand new covers for all five books in the series! They are amazing as are you.

To Faith, my editor and other side of my (somewhat scary) brain. You have been asking me for YEARS for Misha's book. I'm happy to finally be able to give it to you!

To my beta readers, Sandy, Becky, and Lara for reading Misha's story while still in rough stages and giving me your feedback.

And a special thank you to Miranda Liasson, who read Misha's story, told me she loved it, and then told me how to make it even better. Thanks for having my back on this one!

And to my readers who fell in love with Misha from the first pages of Mind Sweeper. I hope Misha's story makes you happy. It did me!

Author's Note

When I started writing the Realm books, I quickly realized that some of the scenes would need to crossover into the other books. Misha, Aleksei and Sergei's stories are interlocking in time—it's a close family, after all—so as you're reading the first three books, you'll probably notice some scenes you've read before...but from a very different perspective. Amazing what you can learn from a new point of view.

I originally planned on only writing a trilogy, but I couldn't get this family out of my mind. So two more books were born! Marrick first appears as Naya's loyal best friend in *Demons Are A Girl's Best Friend* and I wanted to tell this honorable demon's story.

And Boris...this over-the-top father and clan leader has a special place in my heart. How could I not give him a happy ever after?

Prepare for some fun with this crazy but loving family!

Brad –

I know you've probably been wondering why it's taken this long to dedicate a book to you. When I first wrote the character of Misha years ago, he was the quintessential brother character. I decided that when I finally wrote his book, it would be all yours. How could it not be? Misha is loyal, and protective, and funny, with the biggest heart. Sounds like someone I know.

This one's for you, bro.

CHAPTER 1

Misha Sokolov was a demon on a mission.

It was finally time to take the plunge back into the dating game, but unlike the quirky TV show, he didn't need a cheesy game show host or a trio of bachelorettes to make his choice. He had already found his one and only.

It shouldn't matter that they came from different worlds, literally. Love should be able to conquer all—even interdimensional portal jumps.

He glanced over at his teammate Jean Luc, who drove the team van like they were in one of *The Fast and the Furious* movies. Tires squealed as they streaked down Mayfield Road to pick up their other teammate Kyle in Little Italy. With Jean Luc it didn't matter if they were on their way to a case or simply out for a drive, speed was the vampire's constant companion, along with his vampire lady-love, Talia.

"Is something wrong, my friend?" Jean Luc asked as he screeched to a stop in front of Kyle's apartment building, the smell of burned rubber permeating the van.

Misha opened his mouth and then closed it again. How could he explain to Jean Luc...who had only to walk down the street with his long hair and French accent to attract hordes of females...that he, Misha, was nervous about a female? One female—his bachelorette—in particular.

Naya.

His stomach fluttered like a lovesick schoolgirl...or was it the two burritos he'd had for lunch? Either way, Naya was his dream woman. Hell, he'd never seen her human side and he still found her gorgeous. Maybe because her demon side was a purple version of *Xena, Warrior Princess.*

He thought she might be his soul mate, and in his heart of hearts he did believe that love could conquer all, but there was one small problem.

He couldn't talk to her.

He became a bumbling, stumbling idiot whenever he was within a fifty-foot radius of her. Misha Sokolov, who, according to his babushka, was born with the gift of gab. And since his grandmother was over a thousand years old, she would know.

He could talk to females. Had he not already been married three times? True, his first marriage was arranged by his father, but the other two weren't. They didn't work out, but it wasn't because he couldn't talk to them. Natalia, wife number two, would say the opposite, actually. That he was way *too* fond of talking.

He shook his head. His love life, or gaping lack thereof, might be *his* mission, but was not the actual priority right now.

After they picked up Kyle, they were on their way to the demon immigration meeting to work out how to bring the next group of demons to earth from the demon realm.

And Naya would be there.

In approximately one month, the next realm demons would arrive. Even after the first group immigrated with few issues, dissenters in the supernatural community who did not want the realm demons to come to earth had become increasingly vocal. Which meant everything must go according to plan with the next group. Supernaturals, like humans, were not immune to having fear and ignorance cause them to do stupid things.

The back door of the van opened and Kyle hopped inside. Misha smiled at his petite teammate, who was decked out in her usual black jeans, T-shirt, and steel-toed black boots. The color of her hair was often a surprise, although recently she had been keeping it jet black. Today she had a festive streak of red down one side.

She pulled out a bag from behind her back, and he reached for it with glee.

"The bakery! What did you bring me today, little one?"

She handed him the bag. "Three apple strudels. I would've bought more, but there must've been a run on them before I got there."

He opened it and caught a whiff of the cinnamon and sugar wafting up from the bag. Nirvana. "Thank you. This will tide me over until my midafternoon snack." He took a bite of the pastry.

Kyle chuckled. "It's already midafternoon, you know." She gave Misha the once-over before her eyebrows rose slightly. "Don't you look fancy. Is that a new shirt?"

He took a long time swallowing before answering her. "No," he lied before stuffing the rest of the strudel into his mouth and chewing for several moments.

When Kyle opened her mouth to say something else, Misha asked, "Isn't Joe joining us?" If he brought up Kyle's FBI boyfriend, maybe he could distract her.

"Dalton's in Chicago on a case. And don't lie to me, demon. You dressed up for Naya."

Before he could lie to her again, his ringing phone saved him. Dolly was calling from the office.

Misha clicked on the speaker. "Well hello, Dolly," he sang in his bass voice.

"That wasn't funny the first time you did it, Misha, and hasn't been the thousand times since then."

"What can I do for you?" Misha asked, ignoring her scold.

"We've got a call."

"We're on the way to the demon immigration meeting. Can it wait?"

"It's the twins."

Misha sighed. The twins. Dolly didn't need to bother with any further explanation.

If Misha hadn't automated the Bureau of Supernatural Relations filing system a couple of years ago, and they still kept paper files, the twins' folder would be several inches thick, even though they had only been wreaking havoc for a little over a year now. Kyle and Jean Luc normally took the lead when it came to handling the seven-year-old twin boys.

If Misha had to place bets on who would finally expose supernaturals to humans, he would put his money on those two little demons, Matthew and Luke Roberts.

"What have they done now?" Kyle asked.

"I'm sending a picture to Misha's phone."

Misha opened the text a moment later. He'd seen a lot of things during his two hundred sixty-five-year life, but this, *this* was truly disturbing. He looked at the carnage in the picture and shuddered at the waste. He shouldn't be surprised, although this time they had outdone themselves.

Kyle leaned forward and gasped. "Is that blood?"

Misha shook his head. "No, see the chunks of cake on the lawn? It's red icing. Buttercream if I'm not mistaken."

Kyle's eyes widened. "How in the world can you tell it's buttercream?"

He shrugged. "Because buttercream is the only way to go."

"Oh, Mish, you are a freaky food savant. I better call Aleksei and let him know we can't make the meeting."

"That's not going to make my brother happy."

Kyle's eyes twinkled. "That's his constant state with me, so it's all good."

Twenty minutes later they pulled up in front of a small bungalow in Brook Park. When they walked around the house into the backyard, Misha hung back and let Jean Luc take the lead since the twins knew him.

Red and blue balloons hung along the picket fence, with unopened presents perched on the patio table. The two culprits slouched low in lawn chairs, heads bent, presenting their light brown mops of hair instead of making eye contact.

Jean Luc walked over and spoke to them while Kyle tried to corral the remaining boys, who were running around the yard covered with cake debris, hollering about the twins having superpowers.

Thank the Fates the humans at the party were all children. If they had been adults, and had seen whatever the boys did, they would have run screaming *from* the house. Kids were much more accepting of differences.

Misha walked over and motioned to Jean Luc, who joined Kyle in her roundup. Misha crossed his arms and stared down at the twins, wondering if they truly understood how severe the consequences of their actions could be.

He looked over his shoulder and watched while Kyle spoke to the first child. She would clean everything up by using her powers to erase their memories of the incident and replace them with more normal birthday party activities.

And what a cool power to have. Of course he'd been hiding his own powers from almost everyone for centuries, so he had no right to power-envy.

Sometimes he wondered why he was working for the Bureau of Supernatural Relations, but today he understood why his job was so important. He had to protect supernaturals from outing themselves. If humans ever realized supernaturals existed outside of Hollywood, things would get *very* sticky *very* quickly.

Misha glared at the two in front on him. "Tell me what happened."

Culprit number one jumped in first. "I've been practicing picking up things with my mind, and I wanted to show everyone."

Misha was impressed. That was a high-level power, especially in someone so young. "So you picked up your birthday cake in front of your friends?"

He nodded as a glop of blue frosting dropped off his chin onto his jeans. "Yeah. It was a Superman cake, and he can fly, right? But Matty ruined it."

Culprit number two barged into the conversation. "Did not!"

"Did too! You blew up our cake! It's everywhere!" He flung out his arms for emphasis, red frosting spraying out to land in a splatter pattern on the front of Misha's new shirt.

"Take it back Luke, or you're gonna get it," Matty cried.

"No! I'm not scared of you."

Matty dove for his twin, and a cake-smearing wrestling match would have ensued if Misha hadn't grabbed them both by the collar. He lifted the twins up until they were at face level with him, their feet dangling in the air.

"I don't think it's wise to continue on this course."

Luke and Matty's eyes popped wide, and they both blurted, "What are you going to do to us?"

"What do you think I should do to you?"

The twins looked at each other before Luke answered. "You should send us to our room." Matty's head bobbed at his twin's suggestion.

Misha barely stopped himself from laughing at the little con artists. Instead he frowned. "How is that a punishment?"

Matty piped up. "Because we don't get to have any dessert, and we have to think about the consonants of our actions."

"It's *consequences* of your actions. And no one is having any dessert today unless they plan to lick it off their clothes or the swing set."

"Choppers is eating it," Luke said, pointing across the yard.

Misha followed his finger and watched the dog running in circles, trying to lick frosting off its tail.

Before Misha could respond, a small blond woman stomped toward them, half her face covered in blue frosting, reminiscent of the warriors in the movie *Braveheart*…which was a great movie, even if it was too graphic for Misha's taste.

And the comparison to the warriors was an apt one. If the fire threatening to shoot out of her green eyes was any indication, Misha was about to get an earful.

———————

What could possibly go wrong at a seven-year-old's birthday party? That had been Callie's naïve assumption when she agreed to have a small party for her twin boys. When would she ever learn with those two? She wiped the cake off her shoulder, the frosting leaving a blue and more-than-likely-permanent streak on her shirt.

When it came to her boys, nothing was off-limits. They were, to put it mildly, rambunctious...which would be fine if they weren't also demons — literally.

Callie looked around at the twins' latest disaster. The Superman birthday cake had exploded across the backyard, and Matty and Luke were covered so completely that she'd have to hose them off before they could set foot in the house.

The twins were talking to the Bureau of Supernatural Relations, who once again would have to cover for the boys' slipup. She had worked with Kyle and Jean Luc on several different occasions, but the towering demon with the spiky blond hair named Misha had not been as much a part of the earlier incidents.

He usually stood back and let his teammates take the lead, which was more than fine with her. Frankly, his size scared her. She was small and human. No match for his size and strength. She had learned that the hard way with the boys' father.

Jean Luc, who was a nice man — vampire — watched over the boys, so she decided it was safe to run into the house to grab towels and clothes for her twins and the other boys at the party.

When she came out again onto the back patio, she put the clothes down and picked up the hose.

But when she looked across the yard, her heart lurched to a stop. The giant demon Misha had her sons by their collars and was dangling them several feet up in the air.

No one touched her sons.

She rushed toward them. "Put them down," she demanded.

The large demon stared at her. She had never looked directly into his eyes before. They were ice blue, and seemed to pierce her.

"I'll let them go if you promise not to shoot."

What was he talking about? And was that a Russian accent? He looked down, and she followed his glance. She still had the hose in her hand.

"I'll put down the hose when you put down my sons." *What was she saying?* She frowned up at him, and she would have sworn that for a moment he almost smiled. But she had to be imagining things.

He bent down and set Matty and Luke on their feet.

She let go of the breath she was holding.

"Now you," Misha said.

She dropped the hose and pushed the boys behind her. "Why were you manhandling my sons?"

His eyes tightened on her, and he stared for an awkward moment. "I would never harm your sons. We were having a discussion about their actions."

"They will be punished for their actions," she announced in what she hoped was her tough-mom, take-no-prisoners voice.

The hose next to her feet snaked across the lawn on its own. Apparently, her sons, at least, were not intimidated by her drill sergeant voice.

"Luke! Stop it."

Luke's eyes widened into the innocent look he'd perfected at the age of four. "What?"

"Not working this time, bucko. You two stand over by the patio and don't move a muscle."

The boys gave her identical sulky faces before stomping over to the patio. She turned back to Misha as she took a breath to calm her nerves. "I appreciate the team coming here today to help."

He glanced around the yard. "We've never had the pleasure of meeting your husband in the past, but I'm surprised he's not here at the party."

"He's traveling for work," she lied, her heart pounding. "He doesn't get to decide his schedule."

He gazed at her with a shrewd look. "We have been spending quite a bit of time with your boys lately. It might be wise, especially if your husband is away from home frequently, to move to a demon compound until your boys understand how to control their powers."

"I'll talk to him about it when he gets home," she lied again. Should she feel good that the lies were coming easier now? She looked away. "I'd better get the kids cleaned up before their parents arrive. They're not going to be happy their boys' clothes are ruined."

"Kyle will make up a plausible story for the boys when she changes their memories," the demon replied before she rushed away.

Misha watched the little powerhouse hurry back to her sons.

She was hiding something. In spite of the number of incidents perpetrated by her boys, her husband had never been around. She always used the work excuse, but today Misha didn't buy it. He decided to look into it further when he got back to the office and his laptop.

Thirty minutes later the boys and Choppers had been hosed down and memories changed. The kids remembered having the biggest and baddest food fight Northeast Ohio had ever seen. Misha watched as the last parent picked up their son before he climbed into the van with a sigh.

"What is it, big guy?" Kyle asked from the back seat.

He turned back. "Such a tragedy."

"What? The kids are all fine."

"The cake."

Kyle snickered. "I should have known you would fixate on the cake."

"I was right, it was buttercream frosting!"

"How do you know that? Did you lick it off your shirt?"

"No, of course not," Misha said, facing the front again.

Kyle snorted. A few moments later she held her phone between the two front seats while "Taps" played quietly.

"It felt only right to take a moment to mourn the loss of the cake," she smirked.

"Seriously Kyle, you need to stop now," Misha mock-growled at her.

"Fine. But even you have to admit, this case…takes the cake."

Misha shook his head while Jean Luc chuckled as he stomped on the gas pedal and sent the van peeling down the street.

CHAPTER 2

Callie watched her microwave meal spin in a slow, juddering circle on the carousel. She knew how it felt, ending up back where it began without moving forward.

Her friend Jill walked into the break room and opened the refrigerator, pulling out her lunch.

"How was the birthday party?" she asked.

Callie sighed. "Great, until I had to call the Bureau again to clean up another of the twins' messes."

Jill's eyes widened. "What happened?"

Callie looked out the door to make sure none of their coworkers were close by. Most went out to lunch instead of eating bargain microwave dinners, and Jill could probably go with them, but she knew Callie couldn't afford to go out, so she stayed to eat with her.

"They wanted a Superman cake, so I bought them an amazing bakery cake." Amazingly expensive, which meant she would be eating bargain dinners for the foreseeable future. "I set up the picnic table in the middle of the yard and brought the cake out and set it there. The boys were so excited. I told them not to touch it while I ran back inside to grab the plates and forks."

"Oh, no."

"Oh, yes. Luke decided Superman needed to take flight. He picked up the cake with his mind. Not to be outdone, Matty latched onto it with his mind, and they had some sort of mental arm-wrestling match. I was barely in time to see the cake explode all over the kids, the neighbors' dog, and me."

Eyes sparkling, Jill slapped her hand over her mouth before pulling it away a moment later to say, "I'm sorry I wasn't there to help."

"You have your own life, Jill. You can't always be there to clean up my messes. Literally and figuratively. The only good news is that it happened on the weekend. After all the Matty and Luke incidents lately, Mr. Linden has already warned me that I can't miss any more work. But the boys come first."

"Of course they do." Jill pulled a sandwich out of her lunch bag. "But I'm your friend, and I know you can't talk to anyone else about this. You should have called me."

"If it wasn't for you, I wouldn't have known what to do the first time the twins showed their powers in public." Callie shuddered at the memory. The twins were in peewee soccer, and Matty created a fireball and flung it at his brother. Jill was on the sidelines during practice that day, since her daughter was on the team. She was the one who called the Bureau, and Callie met Kyle, Jean Luc, and the intimidating Misha for the first time. When she questioned Jill about what it meant later, her friend explained about the Bureau's mission to protect supernaturals. Jill knew this firsthand since she was a supernatural herself. Not a demon like the twins, but a shape-shifter.

Callie smiled at her. "Thank you for trusting me with your secret."

Jill smiled back, patting Callie's hand. "You need someone on your side."

Did she ever. Callie was completely out of her league with demons and the rest of the supernatural world.

"So Kyle changed everyone's memories?" Jill asked.

"Yeah."

"I don't like your tone. What else happened?"

"Misha questioned me about the twins' father. He wanted to know why he wasn't at the party."

Jill frowned. "What did you tell him?"

"That he was traveling for work." Callie set down her plastic fork, no longer hungry. "I couldn't think what else to say."

"I don't know why you told them he was in the twins' lives to begin with."

"I don't know why I did either, but when the Bureau questioned me the first time I met them, I panicked. I had just seen my almost six-year-old sons conjure *fireballs*. It's not like I was exactly in my right mind at the time." And now she was locked into the lie. And lies caught up with you eventually.

Her stomach rolled. "I think it's time for me to move again."

Jill reached across the table and squeezed her hand. "Don't even think about it."

"I don't know what else to do. I've been here for over a year now, and I've gotten complacent." When the twins were first born, she moved every year until she came to the Cleveland area. She shouldn't have stayed so long. Heck, she should have moved when the twins first showed their powers, but she'd been terrified, and Jill was someone she could rely on.

"Maybe you should tell the Bureau the truth."

Callie's heart thumped. She hadn't even told Jill the whole truth about the boys' father. "I can't."

Jill looked over her shoulder at the open doorway before leaning closer. "I will always be here to help, but I'm not an expert on how to raise demon children. That is way out of my league. Maybe Misha could recommend someone to help you."

Ice-blue eyes flashed in Callie's mind. Eyes that saw too much. She couldn't trust him. Not when it came to the safety of her boys.

———————

Something wasn't adding up. Misha frowned as he set down the almond chicken container and typed away on his laptop. He opened the previous incident files for the twins and reviewed them.

Kyle walked into the back office and looked wide-eyed at the various Chinese food containers on the table. "You haven't finished your almond chicken or your beef and broccoli, and you actually left an egg roll in the box. What's wrong?"

"I'm reviewing the twins' files."

Her eyes widened. "With your photographic memory, since when do you have to review anything?"

"I was not the one who wrote up the case notes, little one. Either you or Jean Luc wrote these reports."

Kyle sat down next to him. "Okay. So, what about the twins has your digestion messed up?"

"I'm trying to find information on the boy's father. Have you ever met him?"

"No. He hasn't been at any of the incidents."

Misha reviewed his computer screen. "I don't even see his name listed."

"What's with the curiosity?"

"I think Callie lied to me about her husband."

"What did she say?" Kyle asked.

"That he was traveling for work."

She shrugged. "Maybe he is."

"No. She's keeping some sort of secret."

Kyle pursed her lips. "Why would she do that?"

"I don't know, but I'm going to find out."

"You and your puzzles." Kyle smiled. "Are you going to keep working on this, or go with us to the meeting?"

Misha shut the laptop lid. He had almost forgotten about the rescheduled demon immigration meeting. If he was lucky, Naya would be joining them.

Forty-five minutes later, they walked into the Shamat demon meeting hall. It had been a while since Misha visited his clan's compound. Misha's father, Boris was already in the room, and he stood and hugged Kyle, kissing her on both cheeks.

"Hello, my daughter," he boomed. "How are you on this fine day?"

"I'm good, Boris." She gave him a sassy grin. "I still can't get over how you used to hate me and now you call me daughter."

Boris tsked at her. "When you saved Misha's life, he claimed you as his *sestra*. Which means you are my daughter." Then he winked. "And I never disliked you, Kyle. You and I just didn't see eye-to-eye on some things."

Misha groaned inwardly at his father's over-the-top style.

Kyle laughed out loud. "Seriously, Boris. You need to run for political office."

"I have enough issues with running the Shamat clan. I don't need to get messed up in human issues as well."

Boris turned to Misha and slapped him on the back. "Son."

Misha's brother Aleksei walked into the room with a Dalmot demon by the name of Kevin Doyle. Aleksei ran the immigration program, and Doyle helped him with the details. Doyle had been Kyle's idea. Leave it to her to recruit a con-demon to help with the many logistical problems involved with bringing realm demons to earth.

As soon as Irina, Misha's babushka, bustled into the room, they took their seats and Aleksei started the meeting.

Before Aleksei could get a few words out, the hair on the back of Misha's neck stood up. He knew what that meant. The portal from the demon realm was opening, and Naya was about to join them for the meeting.

The far wall started to wobble like it was made of Jell-O. A pinprick of light formed in the middle and expanded until the circle was large enough for a person to step through...and step through she did, in all her purple glory. She was gorgeous, even in her black jumpsuit, which was armor-plated to protect her when she was on duty as a member of the portal guard in the realm.

Misha didn't like the idea of her being in danger. Not because she couldn't handle herself. He wasn't that much of a sexist. But he was protective of her. From what Kyle told him, Naya's life in the realm was treacherous. Was it so wrong to want to ease some of that burden?

Naya looked around the table. "Apologies for being late."

"No problem," Kyle said. "Take a load off." She pointed to the empty seat next to Misha.

Misha's heart tried to make a break for it through his rib cage. He shot to his feet and pulled her chair out. Naya's eyebrows rose at the same time a scoffing sound came from the end of the table. Misha glared at his brother.

Aleksei looked at him with raised eyebrows. "Let's continue, shall we?"

Kyle leaned forward. "Where do we stand on the next group of demons?"

Aleksei looked down at his tablet. "We have received petitions to come to earth from over a thousand realm demons."

"How many can we bring through this round?" Misha asked.

"Twenty."

Kyle frowned. "At the rate things are going, this will take years. We have to figure out a way to speed things up."

Aleksei sighed. "We don't have the infrastructure to support a large number all at once. We have to acclimate them to our world, and that takes time and resources. But even though we brought only five over in the first group, we've already increased to twenty."

Boris leaned forward. "No one is questioning the work you've been doing, son. As more realm demons settle on earth, they will help others through the acclimation process. Then we can start bringing larger numbers to earth."

"Agreed," Jean Luc said. "But in the meantime, what can we do to get more resources to help?"

Doyle piped up. "We need an office manager to start with. I'm out of the office working on places for the demons to stay once they've moved out of the halfway house. Aleksei can't keep all the balls in the air by himself."

"Let's put some feelers out to see who we can find," Boris said.

Irina clasped her hands together. "Let me see who might be available through the demon grapevine."

Misha's grandmother had a formidable list of connections and wasn't afraid to call in favors.

"Have we heard any more negative buzz from the dissenters?" Kyle asked.

Aleksei frowned. "Nothing directly at the office. I don't know that it's serious yet."

Doyle shook his head. "I think it is serious. I'm hearing more grumbling from the street. There are many supes who aren't happy with this situation. And it's not only the demon clans. Vamps and shifters are getting nervous too. Letting thousands of powerful demons immigrate to earth could shift the power structure."

Kyle scowled. "What are our options? Make them stay in the realm forever? These demons are generations removed from the ones who rebelled a thousand years ago. Is that how we want to live? I personally still have a soul."

"We are with you, *ma petite*," Jean Luc said in a soothing voice. "But we have to understand that people are scared. There are going to be problems, and we have to be ready to respond."

"The vampire's right," Naya said. "The realm is hard, and demons there are used to fighting to survive. Acclimating the travelers is not merely teaching them about this world, it's also teaching them how to react in it."

Misha nodded. Beautiful and brilliant. He should say something to her. He really should think of something to say—

"What is the mood in the realm?" Aleksei asked.

Darn it! Misha should have asked that.

"For the most part it is cautiously optimistic there. Most demons want to come to earth."

"Most?" Kyle asked. "What about the others?"

Naya placed her hands flat on the table, as if to gather strength from it. "There are others who do not trust what is being offered. They have spent too much time living in the realm. They know the history of our people. They know they were cast aside, and they don't look at this new development as a good thing."

"Are they causing trouble?" Boris asked.

"We have had some skirmishes, but nothing the patrol can't handle. That is why we're there, to keep the peace."

Misha wanted to growl.

Naya looked straight at him and his stomach dropped.

"I would like to growl in frustration as well."

Holy Fates. Had he growled out loud? He glanced at Kyle, whose eyes widened at him before she smirked.

Oh, fu...dge with nuts and caramel swirl on top. *Focus!* Now he'd done it. Naya would think he was certifiable. He couldn't talk to her, but he could sit next to her grunting and growling like an animal.

He was not just blowing his chances with Naya, he was ruining them spectacularly.

CHAPTER 3

Not again. It hadn't even been a week since the exploding cake incident. Callie hung up the phone and dropped her head to her desk with a definitive *thunk*.

"What's wrong?" Jill asked as she peeked around the office cubicle wall.

"The boys are in trouble again at day care."

Jill frowned. "Do you need me to go with you?"

"No. That was Kyle." She lowered her voice. "They've already taken care of things, and the boys are at the Bureau office."

And that scared the crap out of her. She had never been summoned to the office before. What if they were going to tell her she was an unfit mother and try to take them away from her? God, she couldn't handle that.

Callie plopped her head down on the desk again and took a deep breath to stop from hyperventilating. How could she leave work early? But she had to face the music. No matter what, she would fight for her sons.

Jill patted her on the shoulder. "It's going to be okay. Mr. Linden is out of the office, and he's not supposed to be back today."

"I know. I can do this." She stood, grabbed her purse, and smiled even though she didn't feel happy at all.

Jill smiled back at her. "Ah, Callie..."

"Yeah?"

"Before you go, you might want to take that sticky note that says *buy milk and tampons* out of your hair."

Forty-five minutes later, Callie pulled into the parking garage of the Smithson building, and took the elevator to the third floor, where the Bureau's offices were located. By the time she got off the slowest-moving elevator on the planet and stood outside the office door, she was in flat-out panic mode.

Why did they bring her boys to the office? Were they going to send them away? She didn't know if what the boys could do was even normal for a demon.

She was a bad, bad mother. How could she not have found out more about what it meant to be demon?

But if she had asked, it would have clued them in to the fact that the twins' father wasn't in the picture.

Did the Bureau let humans raise demon children on their own?

She sucked in a breath and opened the door, walking into a reception area that looked like something out of a classic movie. The desk was a huge, wooden monstrosity, and the walls were painted an off-white.

Behind the desk sat a gorgeous woman with long blond hair twisted into an intricate knot. She looked her up and down.

"You must be Callie. I'm Dolly. We've spoken on the phone numerous times. It's great to finally meet the woman behind the mini-terrors."

Callie nodded. If Dolly was joking with her, it couldn't be too bad...could it?

Dolly pointed to the door in the back wall. "Go on back, they're expecting you."

Callie opened the door and walked into a room that looked like a second-hand store specializing in seventies furniture. There was a large table made out of some light-colored faux wood. Next to it, her boys sat on a lime green couch. They were coloring, leaning forward in concentration.

Kyle walked over to her. "Hello, Callie."

Luke and Matty's heads popped up and they both blurted, "Momma!"

"What are you two doing?" she asked.

"Coloring," Luke answered. "We're making pictures for you."

"Yeah," Matty chimed in. "We owe you an appleology."

"An *apology*," Kyle corrected him.

Matty's eyebrows raised. "Isn't that what I said?"

"Why do you owe me an apology?"

They boys looked at each other in their silent communication.

"Don't make up a story. Tell me the truth about what happened at day care, please."

Luke spoke first. "Sam wanted to pretend to be Harry Potter, but Matty and I thought one of us should be Harry, and so we had a contest."

Oh Lord, she could only imagine where this was going. "What did you do?"

"Matty and I got drumsticks from the music room and used them as magic wands. Matty shot sparks out of the end of his wand. It was so cool!"

Kyle spoke up. "One of the aides who knows about us called right after she saw it happen. Luckily she was the only adult in the room at the time."

Callie sighed. There was going to be a day when they didn't luck out. She didn't know what would happen when that time came. "You know what you did was wrong, right?"

The boys nodded and looked down at their knobby knees. They were both growing so fast. She took a step toward them but was interrupted.

"We need to talk in my office."

Callie turned toward the deep voice laced with a Russian accent. Misha stood behind her, and his eyes weren't sparkling with humor today.

She looked back at Kyle.

"No problem. I'll stay with the boys while you two talk."

Callie followed Misha down the hall to a room with a desk, chairs, and several laptops. There really wasn't much room for more since Misha himself took up a lot of real estate. He gestured to the chair, but she didn't feel much like sitting down.

Misha continued to stand when she didn't take her seat, and frowned some more. "I need you to clarify something for me. The boys asked me about their powers."

Oh God, oh God. "What did you tell them?"

"I didn't tell them anything. They asked me if they were wizards like Harry Potter, which means they obviously don't know they're demons. How is that possible?"

"I..." Words failed her. Or more accurately, they stuck in her throat.

"Their father didn't tell them what they are?"

Callie shook her head.

"Why not?"

Her lie had come back to bite her. "He's never been in their life."

Misha crossed his arms. "Demons are normally part of their young's lives. Why —"

"He's dead," she blurted.

His eyes flared slightly. "I'm sorry."

She wasn't, but she didn't voice her relief out loud. It would make her sound like a heartless bitch, and she was already worried they thought she was an unfit mother as it was.

"Why did you lie?"

Panic forced its way back into her body, attacking her lungs, making it hard to breathe. She couldn't lose her kids. "I don't have to tell you anything—"

"Callie! Why did you lie?"

She clenched her teeth and swallowed to stop the tears from spilling over before finally saying, "Because I was afraid you would take them away from me. I have no idea what it means to be demon. I can barely control them now, and they're only seven! You can't take them away from me. Please!" Her vision grayed as dots floated in front of her eyes.

Misha grabbed her arms and sat her down on a chair, hunkering down in front of her. "Breathe."

She looked up at him and blinked at his mouth, trying to understand what he was saying.

He enunciated slowly and carefully. "You…need… to…breathe."

She concentrated on inhaling and then exhaling for a few moments until her heart rate slowed down.

"Listen to me. I'm not going to take your sons from you, and anyone who tries to take them will have to go through me first," he growled.

She blinked, surprised at his vehement reaction.

He stood up. "Do you know which clan the boys are from?"

Callie frowned. "Clan?"

"There are twelve clans for the twelve demon types on earth. The boys' father would be from one of them. If we know his clan, we can anticipate some of the changes the boys will go through."

"So they are different than you?"

"Possibly. I can't sense what demon clan they descend from, but it could be that their human side is cloaking it. I can tell you they more than likely come from a high-level clan. Their powers are quite advanced for their age."

"Does it make me a bad mother to admit I wish they were less advanced when it comes to their powers?"

The corners of Misha's eyes crinkled. "No. Most demon children don't get their powers until they're teens or even into their twenties. An older child can more easily understand why they shouldn't show humans their powers. The boys need to know what they are."

Panic spotted her vision again. "No! I have to think this through. I can't simply blurt it out. I don't even know what being a demon means."

"Since I do, I'd be happy to help you explain to them."

He was right, but she needed a little more time. "I need to learn about demons. I have to be prepared to answer questions for them, and be a good mom."

"You already are a good mom, Callie."

"Please give me a little more time. I promise I'll tell them. I'll even let you be there as my backup."

Misha nodded. "Fine. But they're starting second grade in the fall. We've been lucky so far with exposure, but I don't think our luck is going to hold for very much longer."

"I agree. I know this might be a silly question, but do you have some sort of literature or history that I could read about the clans?"

Misha's eyes lit up. "Funny you should ask. I have a PowerPoint training that I use as part of orientation for the Bureau of Supernatural Relations. I could train you."

"Okay, if you have time."

"I'll make time."

Callie's phone rang before she could respond. She pulled it out of her purse. It was Jill. "Sorry, this is work calling. I've got to get this."

She clicked on the phone. "Hello."

"Callie," Jill whispered. "We've got a problem."

"What?"

"Mr. Linden came back to the office, and when he found out you left early he had a little breakdown."

Callie's heart sped up. "How little?"

"Well...he um..."

"Just spit it out, Jill."

"He said something about the last straw and that you're fired. I'm so sorry, Callie. I'm going to talk to him and explain you had an emergency."

Callie closed her eyes. "Don't do that. He might fire you too if you try to speak up for me. Get back to work so you don't get in trouble."

"I'm sorry. I'll call you later. We'll figure out something."

"I'll be fine. I'll talk to you later."

Callie was not going to be fine. She lived paycheck to paycheck now. Panic, her new BFF, curled around her lungs and tried to choke her.

"Callie!"

She opened her eyes and found Misha crouched down in front of her again. "Are you okay?"

She didn't answer.

"I'm sorry to have eavesdropped, but it sounds like you just lost your job."

She blinked back tears. She would not cry on top of everything else. Her life was turning into a train wreck. "I've been missing work a lot lately. My boss warned me, but the boys come first."

Misha's face softened. "Of course they do. Do you want me to speak with him? I can be very persuasive."

She could certainly believe that. "And tell him what exactly? That my sons are demons?"

He pursed his lips. "True. What if I have Kyle change his memories?"

"Great suggestion, but he had a meltdown in

front of the whole office. It's probably gone viral by now."

Misha's mouth quirked up a little on the right side. "Very well. Then we move to plan B. What sort of work did you do?"

"I helped manage sales accounts. I dealt with sales reps and customers to make sure they got their orders."

Misha's eyebrows went up. "Sort of like an office manager?"

"Not really in this case, but I have managed offices in a couple of previous jobs, why?"

Misha beamed, and she blinked at the intensity.

"I may have a job for you that would also provide an additional benefit of learning about demons firsthand. Are you interested?"

She looked into his ice-blue eyes for a moment before nodding. How could she not be interested?

CHAPTER 4

Misha glared at his brother. This in itself was not a new occurrence. But his wish to pummel him—no, that was not a new occurrence either. He took a deep breath and glanced at Kyle, who stood next to him. She gestured for him to continue.

"Why will you not consider Callie for the office manager job?" Misha asked.

Aleksei frowned. "She's human and knows nothing about us."

"Callie may be human, but she knows supernaturals exist. Her twin sons are half demon, and she wants to learn about us. She has the office background to help you as well. You need someone who can dive in immediately, and we can train her about the demon clans along the way."

"I don't know," Aleksei grumbled.

Kyle interrupted. "Aleksei, pull the stick out of your butt and listen for a minute. When we first created the demon immigration office, I took a big risk in suggesting you run it. To be honest, I didn't know if you could table your arrogance and play nice with others. But Misha agreed with me about giving you a chance. If he thinks Callie is a good fit, then let's give her a shot."

Aleksei narrowed his eyes at Kyle for a moment. "It's a good thing you're not our press secretary, Kyle. You are a bit too—"

"Honest?"

Aleksei shrugged. "Very well, I will interview her."

"Great!" Kyle said. "She's in the outer office."

"You want me to interview her now?"

"Yes. Time is money, and we need to work faster to get more realm demons to earth."

Aleksei stood from behind his desk. "On that we agree."

Misha waited to speak until Kyle stepped out of the office. "Be nice to Callie, brother."

Aleksei's right eyebrow cocked up. "Or what?"

Or the pummeling will become a reality. He took a breath. "All I ask is that you give her a chance."

His brother stared at him for a moment before nodding. One minor battle won.

———————

Callie looked up, up, and up into the face of the imposing man. He was as tall as Misha, and wore a suit that probably cost more than several of Callie's rent checks.

Misha introduced them. "Callie Roberts, this is Aleksei Chesnokov. He runs the demon immigration office, and will be interviewing you today."

"Callie. It's nice to meet you," Aleksei said.

His words were polite, but his eyes were guarded. She would have some convincing to do. "Nice to meet you as well."

Aleksei glanced at Misha and then Kyle. "Why don't you two give us some privacy so we can talk?"

Misha winked at her and Kyle squeezed her arm before they both walked out the door.

"They act as if they're leaving you with your executioner," Aleksei muttered.

Callie's eyes widened. "You are a little intimidating, sir."

Aleksei smiled. "Only to my enemies."

And she did not want to end up on that list.

"Now, why don't you take a seat and tell me why I should hire you for this job."

Well, he didn't beat around the bush. She pulled a resume out of her folder and handed it to him. "As you can see, I have worked in a variety of offices. I've organized sales accounts and managed several different kinds of projects."

He reviewed the paper without looking up. "And Misha explained the job to you?"

"Yes. Both he and Kyle. But you're the person I would be working for, so I would like to hear it from you."

"Good answer. The Bureau of Demon Immigration office, or BDI as it is known to the human world, was created after Kyle petitioned the various demon councils to allow demons from the demon realm to move to earth. The demon realm is where five clans were banished after the demon wars took place on earth over a thousand years ago. It is time to bring these demons back to earth. They are descendants of the original clans, and are being punished for something that happened before they were born."

He set down her resume. "None of us truly understood how complicated this immigration process would be. The realm is harsh and primitive."

"I can imagine. Housing, clothing, jobs, language, even teaching them about food, and how commerce is handled."

"Exactly. These demons have been living in a world that doesn't resemble this one in the slightest. We would like to be able to bring more demons to earth, but we need help. Doyle, a demon who works for me, and I have been handling things up to this point, but now we're looking for someone who can handle the office when we're not here."

"Got it."

"We could also use help in automating some of our processes. Right now we're using crude methods." He gestured to the erasable calendars on the corkboard wall across from his desk.

Callie nodded. "There's nothing wrong with having calendars like this so everyone can see what's going on, but there are other things we can use, like phone apps when you're out in the field."

Misha poked his head into the room. "Sorry to interrupt, but Solomon is here and insists on speaking with you."

Aleksei stood. "Sorry, Callie. I have to deal with this. He's been incredibly vocal about his opposition to bringing realm demons here."

"Kyle's talking to him now," Misha said.

Aleksei rushed around his desk. "Damn. That's not good."

Misha frowned. "Is he dangerous?"

"No, I'm more worried about Kyle hurting *him*. Come make sure your teammate behaves herself."

The men left, and after a few minutes Callie got up and reviewed the calendars on the walls. Aleksei wasn't kidding about this job being a logistical nightmare. But the more Callie learned, the more she wanted to help. It would challenge her, and she could learn more about demons so she could explain what they were to her sons.

The phone rang on Aleksei's desk, and she itched to answer it but held her ground until the ringing stopped. A few moments later it rang again. She walked over and picked it up.

"This is Callie. How can I help you?"

"Where's Doyle?" the voice asked.

"He's out in the field. Can I take a message?"

"This is Manny from Sullivan Trucking. We're supposed to be driving a truck of building supplies to the Danver Street address, but we aren't going to make our deadline."

Callie clicked on the speaker phone and then walked over to the calendar to scan it quickly. "You mean the shipment on the twelfth?"

"Yeah."

"That's three days away. How do you know you won't make it?"

"I'm short a man."

Callie looked at the timeline. It already looked tight to finish the house before the demons arrived a month from now. She also saw that Sullivan Trucking was listed prominently on the calendar for other shipments as well.

"I understand what it's like to try to balance a business when you're short-handed, Manny, but we're on a deadline and need those materials. We've sent a lot of business your way recently, and would love to continue the relationship. Isn't there some way to make sure our shipment arrives on the twelfth?"

Silence.

Oh God, what had she done. "Manny?"

"Yeah, I'll figure it out."

"Thanks, Manny. I'll make sure to tell my boss how you stepped up for us on this."

Callie disconnected the phone and a throat cleared behind her. She spun around. Aleksei and Misha stood in the doorway gaping at her. Now she'd done it. How could she get herself out of this gracefully?

"You're hired," Aleksei announced.

"What?"

"You took care of things without being asked, and, from what I heard, you did it well."

"I..." *What just happened?*

"Is that a yes?" Aleksei asked.

"I..."

Aleksei looked over at Misha. "Is she okay?"

"I'm fine," Callie answered. "I'll take the job, if the hours and salary work for me."

Aleksei smiled. "I like you, Callie Roberts. Let's negotiate."

Ten minutes later, Callie walked with Aleksei to his office door. "I'll see you tomorrow morning, then?"

"Yes."

Aleksei opened the door. Misha stood on the other side. "You were right, brother, she's a keeper."

Brother? She looked between the two men. Other than them both being tall and imposing, they looked nothing alike. Where Misha had blondish-brown hair and blue eyes, Aleksei had dark hair and green eyes.

Her elation deflated a bit. Misha walked out of the office building with her.

"Where's Kyle?" she asked.

"She went back to the BSR office. She had a couple of things to get done."

Callie nodded.

Misha stopped and turned to her. "Is something wrong?"

"You didn't tell me Aleksei is your brother."

Misha shrugged. "I didn't think it was relevant."

"Why does he have a different last name?"

"My full name is Mikhail Sokolov Chesnokov. Sokolov is my mother's maiden name. Since I started to work for the BSR in the past I have used Sokolov instead of Chesnokov. Because my father is the Shamat clan leader, we didn't want people to think there was a conflict of interest. In the past year, though, it has become common knowledge that I'm Boris's son."

"Did you convince Aleksei to hire me?"

He chuckled. "My brother has the tendency to do the opposite of what I ask him to do. He hired you because he thinks you will do a good job. He was impressed. So was I, for that matter."

Callie stared at him for a moment to see if he was feeding her a line, but his expression told her otherwise. "Thanks, but I was winging it in there just now. I need to learn about demons fast."

"Let's go to a drive-thru and grab a treat to celebrate your new job. I'm feeling a bit peckish. And then we'll go back to the office, and I'll start your training. I'm sure Kyle will want to help too."

Thirty minutes later, Misha stood in Kyle's office and pleaded with his teammate while Jean Luc looked on with an amused twinkle in his vampire eyes.

"Oh, hell no." Kyle sat in the chair behind her desk with her arms crossed. "You can't make me."

"I brought you a mocha shake," Misha said, holding it out to her.

"And I appreciate that, but no."

Misha took a cautious step toward her. "Kyle, be reasonable."

"I can't watch that PowerPoint presentation one more time, Mish. It's like torture."

"Shh," Misha whispered before looking back at the open door. "Don't say that so loud. Callie is in the main office waiting for us. I told her you would help her with her training."

"Why do you need my help? You're the demon expert."

"You can offer her a unique perspective. It would be helpful for her to hear what you have to say."

Kyle sat up straighter. "Unique perspective, huh?"

Misha glanced over at Jean Luc, who shook his head slightly at him, but it was too late to take it back now.

"Little one, you are the reason why the demon immigration office and her job exists now. Were you not the one to stand up in front of the Demon Council and convince the clan leaders to allow the realm demons to come to earth? You want her to succeed, yes?"

"Of course I want her to succeed. And I'll be happy to offer any help I can provide her." Kyle stood and walked around her desk, grabbed the shake from Misha's hand, and strode out the office door.

Jean Luc chuckled slightly. "Now you've done it, my friend."

"It will be fine."

Two minutes later, Misha realized how not fine it was. He clicked on the keyboard and the first slide appeared. "Pavel demons."

Kyle interrupted. "They're rude and egotistical, think humans are less than."

"They are the highest-level demons on earth," Misha continued, "and they can have a variety of powers. Their demon form is purple skin and yellow eyes."

Callie paled as he spoke. "What do you mean by demon form?"

Misha exchanged a quick glance with Kyle before continuing. "Most of the clans have a human and a demon form. In demon form, our skin and eyes change color."

She swallowed hard. "Can my boys do that?"

Kyle sat down in the chair next to Callie and wrapped her arm around her shoulders. "Since they're half-human they might not be able to change."

Misha also sat down on the coffee table in front of her. "Callie, we'll figure out the best way to tell the boys. Whether they can turn or not, they have powers, and we'll make sure they understand what's happening to them and how to use their powers responsibly."

"Knowing the boys, they'll think it's cool. Okay. Let's get back to the training."

"Are you sure?" Misha asked.

"Yes. The more I understand, the more I can help Luke and Matty."

Misha smiled at her conviction. "Right."

They plowed through several more demon types after Misha explained that there were different levels of demons based on their powers.

"Low, medium, and high levels. Got it." Callie said, more to the notepad in front of her than to him as she scribbled.

"Now on to Haltrap."

"They're egotistical," Kyle said.

Misha sighed. "You have labeled every demon clan as egotistical so far."

Kyle shrugged. "I calls it likes I sees it. Besides, we're at the halfway point. Six down and six to go."

"So, my sons can be from any of these twelve clans?"

"Yes," Misha answered. "But with the powers they're already showing, odds are they're from the three top-level clans."

"And those are?"

"Shamat, Traman, and Pavel."

Callie set down her pen and picked up her notes. "You're Shamat, right?"

"Yes."

"Orange skin with red markings and black eyes."

"That's me in demon form."

"And what are your powers?" she asked, causing his stomach to clench.

"Shamats have a variety of powers as well. Fireballs, strength, telekinesis."

She stared at him for a moment, and he waited for her to ask him again what *his* powers were. Instead she nodded, and he let out his breath and continued with the presentation. Once they finished the slides, Callie continued with her questions.

"So there are still twelve distinct clans? They haven't merged over the years?"

"The different clans on earth haven't been able to mate successfully with each other," Misha explained.

"Obviously they can mate with humans," Callie muttered.

"Yes."

Kyle piped up. "The five clans in the realm aren't able to mate with each other, either, but for some reason the portal guards have been able to mate across clans. We don't know if it has to do with living in the in-between."

"The in-between?"

"Think of it as the border between the realm and earth."

Misha shut the projector off. "The guards originally came from the twelve clans on earth. They volunteered to watch over the expelled demon clans in the realm and stop them from coming back to earth."

Callie's mouth fell open. "They've lived in the demon realm all this time?"

"Yes. And it's not a fun place to visit, let alone live. The demons in the realm are uber-powerful," Kyle said.

"And you're bringing them here?"

"Yes. They've been trapped there for a thousand years earth time—which equates to god-only-knows what in realm years—for something their ancestors may or may not have done."

"Aren't you scared they might go crazy on earth?" Callie asked.

"Possibly. But from what Naya has told me, most of the demons there fight in order to survive."

"Naya?"

"Leader of the patrol. Misha's got a crush on her."

"Kyle!" Misha blurted, praying he wasn't blushing at her words. "Now is not the time."

"It's never going to be the time if you don't actually talk to her."

Misha scowled at her. "I'm sure Callie does not want to hear about Naya. She needs to pick her sons up from day care in a little bit, so we need to get through this presentation."

Kyle narrowed her eyes at him. "Right."

He didn't need to think about Naya right now, or the fact that Kyle was not going to let it rest any time soon.

CHAPTER 5

Kyle barged into Misha's office, which he would have normally chastised her for if she hadn't been wearing such a worried look on her face. "What's wrong, little one?"

"Someone vandalized one of the demon halfway houses."

Misha stood and rounded the desk. "Where's Jean Luc?"

"He and Talia are on their way there. I told them we'd meet them."

Thirty minutes later they pulled up to the demon halfway house. On the outside, the small house looked fine.

But once they entered the building, the damage was quickly evident. The walls were splattered with paint, and the couch and chairs in the living room had been torn open, the cotton padding strewn around the room.

Jean Luc and Talia walked into the room from the back hall.

"Did you find anything?" Kyle asked.

"The kitchen table is destroyed. Luckily, they did not tear the cabinets apart," Jean Luc replied.

Talia scowled. "Chickenshits, the whole lot of them."

Misha would have smiled at Talia's blunt comment if the situation didn't make him so angry.

She continued. "Sneaking in here and destroying this house isn't going to stop demons from coming to earth."

"Damn straight," Kyle barked.

Misha frowned. "I was supposed to install cameras some time during the next week. I wish I had done it sooner. We might have been able to identify the vandals."

Aleksei burst into the room, took one look around, and let out a torrent of Russian curses that even Misha found surprising.

His swearing finally petered out, and he closed his eyes. "How bad is it?"

Jean Luc answered. "Mostly this room and the kitchen table. The bedrooms were empty, so they didn't have anything to destroy."

Aleksei sighed. "Luckily the beds weren't scheduled to be delivered yet, or they would have destroyed them too. Callie has them scheduled for delivery in two days." Aleksei hit a button on his phone, and Doyle's voice came across the speaker.

"How bad is it?"

"Not too bad. Bring the cleaning crew with you and a couple gallons of paint for the living room."

"On the way," Doyle replied before hanging up.

Misha took a step toward his brother. "You didn't leave Callie alone at the office, did you?"

"She went home for the night. Do you think they might attack the office?"

"I don't know what to think, but we need to be careful, so things don't escalate. Maybe it isn't a good idea for Callie to work for you."

Aleksei's eyes tightened on Misha. "I don't think that is your decision to make, brother."

Kyle looked between the two of them and turned to Misha. "I don't normally agree with Aleksei, Misha, but I think he's right. It's Callie's decision where she wants to work."

Misha frowned as he looked at the paint on the walls. "I don't like it. We need to figure out who is behind this."

Kyle nodded. "Agreed. Let's go canvas the street and see if the neighbors saw anything today."

"You and Talia go door-to-door," Misha said. "I'll get the cameras out of the van and have Jean Luc help me set them up now."

Misha didn't think he was overreacting. He had seen enough over the years to know that this was more than likely to escalate, and he didn't want anyone to get hurt.

Misha's phone rang, waking him up. He grabbed it, expecting another call from the BSR. He hadn't been sleeping long since leaving the halfway house. Had something else happened? He looked at the screen. It was Callie.

"Callie?" He looked over at the clock. Three a.m. "Is something wrong?"

"I'm sorry to call in the middle of the night, but it's Matty. He's not feeling well. He has a fever, I think. It's 105. What temperature is a fever for demons?"

Misha threw the covers off and scrambled out of bed. "103 is our normal temperature."

"I don't know what to do. I was going to take him to the hospital, but I was scared they might run tests on him and find out he's not a hundred percent human."

He pulled on a pair of pants. "I'll be right there. We'll take him to one of our doctors."

She blew out a harsh breath. "Thank you."

He threw on a shirt and jeans and crammed his feet into shoes before grabbing his keys and running down the steps of his apartment building and out to his car.

He sped out of the parking lot and down the street. Luckily, he was close to an on-ramp to the interstate, and it wouldn't take him too long to get to Callie's house. He clicked the phone button on his steering wheel. "Call Sabrina."

A few seconds later the call connected and their team doctor answered. "What's happened, Mish?"

"I've got a sick child I need your help with." Misha heard rustling, before Sabrina spoke again. "Tell me the details while I get dressed."

"He's seven. Half human, half demon. He's running a temperature, 105 the last time I talked to his mother."

"Where are they?"

Misha rattled off the address. "Can you meet me there? Callie is worried. Said the twins have never been sick before."

"There are two of them?"

"Yes, although Luke is fine as far as I know."

"I'm on my way."

"Sabrina, the boys don't know they're demons. They know they have powers, but their mother hasn't told them the truth yet."

"Got it. I'll see you in about thirty minutes. In the meantime, the priority is to get his fever down, especially if it's higher than 105."

Misha hung up and sped along the highway. Demons were normally hearty and didn't get sick easily, but since the boys were half human, anything could happen.

Fifteen minutes later he pulled into Callie's driveway and ran up the stairs onto the porch. Misha knocked on the door, forcing himself not to break it down.

A young voice asked. "Who is it?"

"It's Misha."

Luke opened the door and stepped back, his eyes wide.

"Where's your mom?"

"She's with Matty in the bedroom." Luke ran toward the back of the small house and Misha followed him.

Callie sat on the bed next to Matty, mopping his pale face with a washcloth. Misha set his hand on Matty's forehead. He was definitely hot. "Have you checked his temperature lately?"

"It's 107," Callie answered with a catch in her voice.

"Luke, can you do me a favor, big guy?"

"Yes."

"I need you to go in the bathroom and fill the tub up with water. Cold water. Can you do that for me?"

Luke looked at his mom.

"Go on, honey."

Luke ran out of the room.

Misha walked to the other side of the bed.

"What are you doing?"

"I'm going to help you strip him. We'll put him in the cold water to bring his temperature down."

"Shouldn't we be going to the doctor?"

"She's on her way here."

Callie's eyes glistened, and Misha's chest tightened. He reached for Matty, and she tensed.

"Let me help, Callie."

She nodded, and he helped her pull off his Iron Man pj's. "Tell me how you're feeling, Matty."

The boy blinked glassy eyes at him. "Mr. Misha?"

"Yep, it's me, Matty. Tell me where it hurts."

"My head."

"Anywhere else?"

"No."

"Okay. Let's get you in the bathtub." Misha scooped him up and let Callie lead the way.

Luke was in the bathroom, sitting on the side of the tub and watching the water rise. He jumped up when Misha walked over.

"Is the water cold, Luke?"

Luke put his hand into the water and nodded.

"Okay, buddy. Let me get Matty into the tub."

Misha placed him slowly into the water, but Matty still gasped at the cold. "Sorry, Matty, but it will help you feel better."

Luke sniffed beside him, tears pooling in his large green eyes. Eyes very much like his mother's.

"Luke. Can you please go wait at the front door? The doctor is going to be here any minute. She is a pretty blond lady named Sabrina. Will you bring her back to the bathroom when she gets here?"

"Yes, Mr. Misha."

Callie knelt down beside Matty and held his hand while Misha scooped up the cold water and poured it over the boy's small shoulders. Matty whimpered, and Misha bit back the Russian expletive that threatened to burst from him.

"I know it's cold, buddy. Just a little while longer, okay?"

Matty nodded, and Callie ran her fingers over his light brown hair, brushing it back from his forehead.

"He needs a haircut. They both do. I was planning to take them soon," she said as tears streaked down her cheeks.

Misha wanted to gather her, Matty, and Luke into his arms and protect them from all the bad things in the world, but he couldn't do that.

"Doctor Sabrina Miller is an amazing doctor. She'll know what to do, Callie."

As if summoned by his statement, Misha heard voices in the hall. A moment later Luke appeared, holding hands with Sabrina, pulling her into the crowded bathroom. She set her bag on the counter and motioned for Misha to back up so that she could get close to Matty.

"What's going on?" Sabrina asked.

"His fever went up to 107. He's complaining that his head hurts too," Misha said.

Sabrina knelt next to Callie. "I'm Sabrina. I'm going to take care of your son." Sabrina leaned closer to Callie and spoke softly. "What clan are your boys from?"

Callie shrugged. "I don't know."

Sabrina didn't even blink. She pulled the stethoscope from around her neck and placed it in her ears. "That's okay. Most illnesses carry across the clans, which means it's treated the same way."

Sabrina smiled at the shivering boy in the tub. "Hello, Matty. I'm going to listen to your chest now." She listened for a bit before helping Matty sit up so she could place the stethoscope on his back. "Take some deep breaths for me, Matty."

She pulled the stethoscope out of her ears. "Your heart and lungs are strong. Let's see what your temp is now."

Misha handed her the thermometer off the counter, and she held it in Matty's ear until it beeped. Misha held his breath as she looked at the monitor. "It's gone down. 106. Can you stay in the water a couple more minutes for me, Matty?"

"Yes. Are you an angel?" Matty asked. "You look like an angel."

Sabrina chuckled. "No, I'm not an angel."

"Then how did you know my name?"

"Your brother Luke told me. I'm a doctor."

Matty looked up at her with such serious eyes. "I'm not normal. Is that why I'm sick?"

Callie sobbed once, before covering her mouth.

Sabrina rested her hand on his shoulder. "You're right. You're not normal, Matty. You're very, very special. Now tell me about your head. Misha said it hurts. Where does it hurt?"

Matty lifted his hand up and placed it on his right temple. "Here, behind my eyes."

Sabrina pulled a small penlight out of her pocket. "I'm going to look in your eyes for a moment."

She flashed the light over Matty's eyes, and he flinched.

Sabrina sat back and patted Callie on her arm. "I know what's wrong. He's going to be fine once I get the right medicine into him."

Thank the Fates! Misha wanted to shout the roof off or dance around the house. Instead he looked over at Callie's relieved face. For now, that was celebration enough.

———————————

Callie spent most of her life in a perpetual state of anxiety, but what just happened scared the living daylights out of her. Her chest was so tight that she couldn't suck enough oxygen into her lungs.

Matty was settled back in his bed, sleeping. The doctor had given him a shot, and not too long after that he fell asleep.

The doctor reached for the thermometer and checked him again. "He's 104, almost back to normal."

"Thank God. What's wrong with him?"

"It's a common illness that used to affect demon children before we came up with an inoculation. I want to inoculate Luke too. Otherwise, he'll probably get sick as well."

"I didn't know what to do. They've never been sick before. I used to take them to a regular doctor before I realized a year ago that they're half demon. Their temperature used to be 98.6 when they had their physicals."

Sabrina nodded. "Once their powers started to manifest, it probably jumpstarted their demon side, which is why their temperature changed."

"I should have found out about what it means to be demon. I could have prevented Matty from being sick."

"Don't beat yourself up too much, Callie. You didn't know about the supernatural until your sons' powers appeared, right?"

"Yeah. They conjured fireballs a couple weeks before their sixth birthday."

Sabrina's mouth fell open. "Those little over-achievers!"

"That's what Misha said. I didn't know what was going on. Thank goodness my friend Jill was able to explain it to me. She's a shifter, and called in the team to cover up the mess."

Sabrina frowned slightly. "Why didn't Misha explain things to you back then?"

Callie watched Matty sleep for a few moments before responding. "I lied to the team and told them I was married. They thought my demon husband was in the picture and I knew what was happening. But I was clueless and scared that they would take my sons away from me if they knew I was alone."

Sabrina placed some of her items in her doctor's bag. "Perfectly understandable. You were protecting your sons." She pulled out a small bottle and syringe.

"Luke is not going to be happy about getting a shot."

Sabrina smiled at her. The woman was gorgeous. Were all female supernaturals supermodels? "Why don't you break the news to him? I'll sit here with Matty until you come back."

She hesitated for a moment.

"I won't leave him, I promise."

Callie stepped out of the bedroom. She stopped in the hall when she heard Luke's voice.

"Is Matty going to be okay?"

"Yes." Misha answered.

"I was so scared. I didn't know what to do."

"You did fine, Luke."

"I couldn't help Matty or Momma."

"You did. You let me into the house while your momma was helping Matty. You also helped with the tub, and brought the doctor to us. You did everything we asked you to do, little man."

Callie peeked around the hall corner. Luke was crying and turned away from Misha.

"Don't hide your tears, Luke," Misha said softly.

Luke turned around and wiped his tears with the back of his hands.

"Don't ever be afraid to cry. Real men cry. Got it?"

Luke lunged for Misha and flung his arms around the large man's neck. Misha's eyes widened, and he wrapped his arm around Luke. After a moment of hesitation, Misha kissed the top of her son's head.

In that gut-wrenching moment, Callie knew her sons needed a male role model in their lives. It was time to tell the boys the truth about who they were and hope that Misha's clan was as accepting as the large demon her son was clinging to.

Tears trickled down Callie's cheeks, but she was finally, finally able to take the first deep breath in what felt like years.

CHAPTER 6

Misha took a deep breath. He needed to convince Callie that the boys deserved the truth—sooner rather than later. But he was afraid he had a fight on his hands.

She was stubborn, and extremely protective of her sons. Not that she didn't have a right to be. Raising them alone had to be difficult, and that wasn't even taking into account the fact that they were coming into their powers.

It was hard to believe the boys were already showing their powers at the age of seven. That had to mean something. As he had explained to Callie, at the very least it meant they were from a high-level demon clan. Maybe they were even Shamat, and then his father might be willing to adopt them into the clan. But he doubted it could be that easy.

Misha opened the door to the demon immigration office and stepped into a bustle of activity. Doyle had a Bluetooth speaker hanging over his ear, and he was chatting away to someone on the phone about the need for more clothing and supplies. In the midst of doing that, he was watching several males load boxes on dollies to take outside. Before Misha could ask, Doyle pointed toward the back room as if he knew what Misha wanted.

The room Doyle pointed out was a conference room. Aleksei and Callie sat at a table, their heads close together, going over a stack of papers.

It looked like it hadn't taken long for his brother to accept Callie's help. On the one hand Misha should be happy that his suggestion had worked, but on the other hand they were sitting *awfully* close together. Aleksei was a bit of a player, having dated a considerable number of females in the past. Callie did not need to be the next one on his long list of love 'em and leave 'em.

Misha cleared his throat, burying the growl that wanted to erupt. They both looked up at him.

"I'm surprised to see you here, brother," Aleksei said. "What can I do for you?"

"Actually, I'm here to see Callie."

Callie's eyes widened. "Has something happened to the boys?"

Misha held up his hands. "The boys are fine. I was wondering if you have time to grab a bite to eat?"

Callie's mouth dropped open slightly, before she seemed to collect herself. "Um...we're kind of busy right now."

Aleksei pushed back from the table with a smile. "I was about to suggest that we have food brought in."

Misha bit back another growl. "I'm sure you can spare her for a little while, brother."

Aleksei's smile grew, the condescending bastard. "You have been working really hard, Callie. Why don't you take a little break?"

Callie looked between Aleksei and Misha before finally nodding. "Let me go get my purse."

Callie walked out of the room, and Misha spun to face his brother. "How is Callie working out?"

Aleksei straightened the papers on the table for a drawn-out moment before looking at Misha. "She's great. Smart, a hard worker, and not afraid to get her hands dirty. I'm glad you suggested her."

Misha looked over his shoulder to make sure Callie had not come back. "It looked awfully cozy in here. Remember that Callie's vulnerable right now."

Aleksei's smile disappeared, and he stood slowly. "What exactly is that supposed to mean?"

Misha leaned over the table. "It means you should keep this relationship professional."

Aleksei's eyes narrowed. "I'm not the one making it personal."

"I'm ready," a voice announced behind Misha.

Misha turned to find Callie gripping her purse and frowning. *How much had she heard?*

"Do you want us to bring you something back, Aleksei?" Callie asked.

"No, don't worry about me. You two have a good lunch." Aleksei straightened his jacket and marched toward his office.

Misha gestured toward the door. "Shall we?"

They walked out of the office building and turned right and down the street. They hadn't gotten two steps before Callie spun around, and Misha nearly crashed into her.

Her eyes widened as she looked up at him. She seemed to lose her resolve for a second, but then she shook her head slightly and put a hand on her hip.

"What were you and Aleksei talking about? You both looked upset."

Misha shrugged. "Nothing. Old business between brothers. So, what do you want to have for lunch? I thought since it's so nice outside we could order something from one of the food trucks down the street and sit on a bench."

"That sounds good."

Misha led her down the street and stood back as she reviewed the menu at the first truck. "Do you see anything you want?"

She stepped up to the window. "Can I please have a chicken taco?"

"Sure. What, about you Misha? You want your regular?"

Misha tapped the window counter. "Yep, Bill. And throw in an order of empanadas for the lady."

"Got it."

"You know the food truck guy?" Callie asked as he led her to a bench.

"I know most of the food truck guys. The good food trucks, anyway. There's something special about people who can cook so well in a kitchen on wheels. Have a seat. Bill will holler when the food's ready."

She settled on the bench. "What do you want to talk about?"

Misha sat down and swallowed hard before jumping into the deep end of the demon pool. "I think it's time to tell the twins the truth."

Callie opened her mouth, but Misha held up his hand. "Please let me finish before you argue with me." When she didn't say anything, he continued. "I know you've been scared to tell them the truth before, and I understand why. You were alone and didn't understand what this meant. But now you have our clan to help you and the boys, yes?

"Right now, all Luke and Matty know is that they have these superpowers that no one else does. Of course they're going to explore their powers. It's a natural part of growing up. They need to know there are more like them in this world. Until they know what they are, and why it's important to hide what they can do from humans, and the consequences if they don't, they won't stop. And it just can't continue, for their safety and the safety of all supernaturals."

She looked up at him for a moment in silence before finally saying, "I agree."

"I know it's hard to take the next step, but— Wait... Did you just agree?"

"Yes. I made the decision to finally tell them when Matty was sick."

"Why didn't you say so?"

Callie's mouth quirked up at the sides. "Because you told me to let you talk, and you obviously had practiced the speech, so I wanted to let you finish it."

Misha laughed. "You're right. I practiced. Thank you for letting me get it off my chest."

"You're welcome."

"When do you plan to tell them?" he asked.

She looked down at her hands. "When I get my nerves under control."

"Sometimes it helps to practice what you're going to say first."

She chuckled. "As you just showed me."

"Misha! Order up!"

"I'll be right back." He walked over, grabbed two trays, and brought them back to the bench.

Callie gaped. "Who is going to eat all that food?"

Misha looked down at the six tacos and order of empanadas on his tray before handing her the other tray. "Me. The tacos are small. I might have to stop at one of the other trucks for another course."

"Are you kidding?"

He chuckled. "No. Try the empanadas. You'll love them."

She took a bite and her eyes widened. "These are great."

"I know." He picked up one of his tacos and took a bite. They ate for a moment in companionable silence. "Is Matty feeling better?"

Callie smiled. "Yes. Both he and Luke have recovered from the other night. They are actually spending the night at my friend Jill's house tonight. Her family are shifters, so I don't have to worry about the boys messing up in front of humans."

"So you'll be alone, yes?"

"Yes."

"Perfect. Why don't I come to your house and you can practice on me tonight?"

"What?" Callie squeaked before choking on her food.

"Are you okay?" Misha asked, setting his tray on the bench next to him.

She nodded. He opened the water bottle on her tray and handed it to her. She took a sip, and then another. Finally, she wiped her eyes with her napkin.

"Sorry, it went down the wrong way." She cleared her throat. "What were you saying about…practicing on you?"

"Yes. You can practice your speech with me before you tell the twins."

She looked down at her tray. "Right, the speech. I'm sure you have something more important to do with your free time than spend it with me."

"No," he said. "I have no plans tonight. I'd love to help. Anything for the boys."

CHAPTER 7

Callie straightened the pillows on her couch, again, and pondered her ridiculousness.

She knew better than to get her hopes up. Had she not sworn off men until the boys went off to college? Yet here she was, thinking she had a chance with Misha. Yes, he was a caring person, with a heart as big as he was. But he wasn't interested in her. He was worried about her boys' well-being.

She was happy to have someone taking an interest in her sons, and why wouldn't he? Matty and Luke were adorable when they weren't blowing things up.

She could admit, however, that she was a little sad that Misha didn't see her as more than the boys' mom.

But then he was already in love with Naya, right? She was a demon guard, which meant she was tough and could take care of herself. Plus, she had sacrificed a lot by spending her life in the demon realm. And odds were she was gorgeous, because that's how Callie's life worked.

And did she want to get involved with another demon? On the one hand she was a little scared about the idea of dating a demon. Sure, she had been involved with a demon in the past, but she didn't know he was a demon at the time, so did that really count? On the other hand, Misha was nothing like

Mark, and he cared for her boys. To him, she was the invisible one.

And now she had traveled full circle, and was back at the beginning of her dilemma.

She punched the pillow harder than necessary.

Misha was a friend. Nothing more. And she should be grateful that he was willing to help her explain things to the boys.

Callie sat down and ran her hands over her jeans before standing up again. She was acting like a teenager on her first date. Or what she thought a teenager should act like, anyway. She had grown up way too fast to enjoy any type of normal childhood.

The doorbell rang, and she walked over and answered it, stepping back to let Misha enter the room.

He smiled down at her. "Hello Callie."

"Misha." She gestured to the couch. "Would you like something to drink?"

"I'm fine right now." He walked over and sat down on the one end while she sat gingerly at the other.

Misha rubbed his hands together. "Okay. Let's talk about the best way to tell the boys."

She swallowed. "I don't know where to begin. I can't simply blurt out that they're demons."

"I agree. I would start with talking about their powers, and how having powers makes them special. Let them know they're not alone."

"It would help if I knew what type of demons they are."

Misha rested his forearms on his thighs and leaned forward. "It would be easier. I've been thinking about that. Why don't you tell me about the boys' father, and I can more than likely trace him back to a clan."

Ice shot up her spine. Should she trust him with the truth? She had spent the last seven years on the run, trying to protect her sons.

"I…don't know much about him." She clenched her hands together. "That sounds awful. I don't want you to think that I slept with a stranger." Although looking back now, she had, hadn't she?

Misha moved closer. "I'm not here to judge you, Callie. I'm here to help."

"What do you want to know?"

"Let's start with a name. You'd be surprised how much I can find out with only a name."

"Mark Stewart. I met him in Lexington. There was a bar on the first floor of the building where I worked. My coworkers and I would go there for drinks on Friday nights. Mark was there one night. He asked me on a date, and we started seeing each other.

"He was kind of mysterious, and I bought into the romance of it. He treated me well. But…"

"But what?" Misha prompted.

"But I overheard him talking on the phone one night. He was talking about finishing the job and going on to the next on the list. Whatever that meant. And the more I thought about it, the more him being so mysterious was no longer sexy and ended up being kind of scary instead.

"I mean, I didn't know much about him at all. He said he didn't have any family and he traveled around for work, but he never really explained what he did."

"Did you ask him about it?"

"When I asked him more about his childhood, he got angry. I wondered if he was in the Mafia or a gang or something. I told him I didn't want to see him anymore, and he laughed and said I didn't get to decide when our relationship was over.

"One night I came home and found him in my apartment. He announced he was living with me until he finished his job. I told him to leave, and he refused."

Misha frowned. "Did you call the police?"

Callie stood up and walked over to the fireplace, facing away from him. Did she want to bare her soul to him? She took a deep breath and let the words come. "I grew up in a house where my mom's boyfriend abused her. I saw what my mom went through. Nothing worked to get rid of her boyfriend until…" She stopped talking and looked at the picture of her sons on the mantle.

He walked up next to her and she jumped. He was stealthy for a big man.

He looked down at her. "Until what, Callie?"

"Until he killed her."

He placed his hand lightly on her shoulders. "I'm so sorry."

She cleared her throat. "I swore I wouldn't become my mother, but I had to a certain degree. Mark hadn't hit me yet, but he had taken over my life, controlling what I did and who I spent time with. I started to make plans to run away. I hid money when I could, along with a small bag I could grab when I had the chance to run."

"What happened?" Misha asked.

She swallowed. "I came home after work and found him in the back alley of our apartment building, lying in a pool of blood. He told me not to call the police. Then he said he was dying, and the people who had hurt him would be after me next.

"I asked him why, and he said they couldn't risk allowing me to live. He placed his hands on me and told me to stay safe." A tear ran down her cheek and she wiped it off. "I watched him die. I wanted to get away from him, but I didn't want him to die."

Misha placed a finger under her chin and lifted her face until she looked into his startling blue eyes. "It's not your fault. It sounds like he was into something illegal."

"I went to my apartment. The place was trashed. I ran into the bathroom and got sick, and when I stood up and looked at myself in the bathroom mirror, I saw Mark's bloody handprints on my shirt across my stomach. I changed out of my bloody shirt, grabbed my bag and the money I had hidden and left that night."

"How did you survive?" he asked.

She smiled, even though her heart pounded at the memory. "I had seen enough movies to know I couldn't use my credit cards or license to go anywhere. So I sold my car for cash and hitchhiked to Chicago. I got a job where they didn't ask for my ID and paid me under the table, and I found someone who made fake IDs.

"I thought I was safe in Chicago, but I started to get the feeling that someone was following me. I took off again and changed my name to Roberts."

Misha dropped his hand from her chin. "You're ingenious."

"I was desperate. Especially when I realized I was pregnant."

"How did you take care of yourself during your pregnancy?"

"I moved to a small town in Indiana and told people my husband was a soldier who had died in the Middle East. The people were so sweet there. I hated lying to them, but I couldn't have survived without them during the months after the boys were born. I moved on from there a year after they were born."

"And you've been running ever since, yes?"

She nodded. "I couldn't risk our safety. I moved once a year until the boys showed their powers right before their sixth birthday, and it threw me for a loop."

"Mark never told you he was a demon." Misha's ice-blue eyes darkened. "You were in a relationship with him, and he didn't tell you he was demon."

"That's right."

"Even after he became sexually active with you and you could get pregnant?"

"But I was on the pill. He knew that."

Misha growled.

"What?"

"The pill does not prevent conception with demons."

She paced the small living room. "So he was trying to get me pregnant on purpose."

"I would say yes."

"Why?"

Misha cleared his throat. "Demon females in some clans have a hard time conceiving. It could be that he was trying for children with you."

She shuddered, thinking back to the bloody handprints on her stomach. "The day he died, do you think he knew I was pregnant?"

"Possibly. He might have sensed the twins' energy."

"And if he had lived? What would he have done?"

"Honestly? He might have taken the boys."

More tears ran down her face. "He was using me as an incubator."

Misha walked toward her, and she flinched before she could stop herself. He held up his hands and took a step back from her. "I didn't mean to startle you."

"I'm okay. It's just a lot to take in." And wasn't that the understatement of the century…hell, the millenium?

"Yes. And I want to ensure you that, unlike Mark, most demons are good. My clan is good, and your sons are good."

She blinked up at him. His mouth drew a tight line of determination, and his expressive eyes seemed to suck her in to believing him.

"I don't understand any of this. How can I possibly explain it to the boys?"

"What do the boys think happened to their father?"

"I told them he died before they were born."

"Which is true. You don't need to tell them anything else about him except that he was a demon, which is where they got their powers."

"Right." She wiped her sweaty palms against her jeans again. "Enough about my sordid past. Let's figure out what to tell the boys."

Misha opened his mouth as if to say something else, but closed it and nodded.

Callie sat down again and exhaled slowly to calm her thudding heart. She would do everything in her power to make sure her boys grew up to be good. It was time to stop running and stand up for her family. The boys deserved to know who they were.

CHAPTER 8

Misha was not a violent demon on most occasions, but right now he wanted to punch something. If only the demon he wanted to injure wasn't already dead.

Misha pulled into the office parking garage and turned off his car. Mark Stewart. Odds were his name was an alias, but Misha was a determined demon when on a mission.

And he was now on a mission.

A true mission that involved helping an amazing woman and her sons. Callie's bravery awed him. To take care of her sons on her own with no support system… And to do this while on the run.

He had stayed with her for another hour after her revelations, talking about how best to tell Matty and Luke the truth about their powers. He lingered as long as he could, until she finally said she was exhausted and wanted to go to bed.

Misha was far from exhausted. He had to do *something*. He would spend the night trying to find out more about the bastard demon who hurt Callie. He headed toward the elevator, but then thought better of it, taking the stairs instead. Kyle called the elevator a death trap, and while a falling elevator wouldn't kill him, he didn't want to risk getting stuck in it. He had work to do.

He ran up the stairs and unlocked the front door since it was after work hours. To his surprise, he heard voices in the back office. He opened the door to find Kyle, Jean Luc, and Talia sitting at the table. Jason, their other teammate stood in the kitchenette making a pot of coffee.

"What did I miss?"

Jean Luc shrugged in his laid-back, French way. "A fight between two shifter teenagers sparring over the same girl."

"Why didn't you call me?" Misha asked.

Kyle answered him. "We had it under control. And we knew you were meeting with Callie tonight. How did it go?"

Misha gritted his teeth. "Fine, other than I want to kill the boys' father, but I can't."

Kyle exchanged a glance with Talia and Jean Luc before leaning forward. "You're too honorable to do something like that."

"Honor has nothing to do with it. He's already dead."

"Then you got your wish without having to risk supernatural jail time."

Jason handed him a cup of coffee. "Not sure if you need the caffeine right now, but here you go."

"Thanks." He took a sip of the coffee.

Jason set a mug in front of Kyle and sat down at the table. "Why don't you tell us what happened? I'm a little behind on the story."

Misha launched into the story, bringing him and the rest of the team up to speed. When he finished, he looked around the table at his teammates who wore a variety of angry looks.

"Now I know why you want to kill him," Kyle said. She gripped her mug so tightly, Misha was afraid she would shatter it.

"Yes, little one. I'm going to see if I can find out more about him, so we can determine what clan the boys originate from."

Kyle sat up straighter. "The clan can't have them back."

Misha scowled. "If I do find out who this Mark Stewart is, I don't plan to let anyone know about the boys. That is Callie's call."

Talia leaned forward. "What can we do to help?"

"I'm going to start looking through the paranormal database, as well as the human law enforcement databases, to see if I can find out anything about him."

"I can look in the paranormal database," Jean Luc said.

"And I can do some digging as well with my bounty hunter contacts," Talia announced before standing.

Kyle clapped her hands. "Sounds like an all-nighter to me."

"You don't all have to stay."

"We don't have anything better to do," Jason said. "Time to order pizza."

Misha's stomach growled. "Can we order garlic bread too?"

Jason smiled. "Anything you want, big guy."

Misha nodded at his teammates. "Very well. Let's get to work."

Three hours, two large pizzas, and an order of garlic bread later, the team was no closer to finding Mark Stewart than before.

Misha sat back and pinched the bridge of his nose. It was like the man was a ghost. Of course, they had almost nothing to go on other than a name that was obviously an alias.

Kyle sat down next to him at the table. "You okay, Mish?"

"I'm frustrated, little one."

Jean Luc closed the laptop he was working on and set his hands on top of the lid. "Let us talk through where to go next."

"We don't have anything to go on," Misha responded.

"We know he was in Lexington eight years ago. There is a small group of Baltran who live on the outskirts of the city."

"True," Misha said. "But they're not high-level. The powers the boys have already are high-level. It's hard to believe their father could be Baltran."

Kyle tapped her fingers on the table. "They're also half human. Maybe that's playing a part in their powers."

"I would think that would weaken them," Misha responded.

Kyle stood. "We should talk to Sabrina. Who knows what human DNA could do when mixed with demon? Look at me."

"Very true," Jason countered. "There is only one Kyle McKinley. Thank goodness."

Kyle glared at him. "Look who's talking, shifter boy."

Misha glanced over at Jason to see how he reacted to Kyle's jibe. It hadn't been too long ago that Jason found out he was half-shifter, and he hadn't taken it well at first.

Jason rolled his eyes. "Touché, demon-girl."

Jean Luc interrupted before the two could continue their argument. "We should bring Sabrina into this anyway. She could probably take some blood samples and test to see if she can identify their clan."

"That isn't foolproof," Kyle said. "It didn't work with me."

"True, but it is still worth pursuing."

"I'll talk to Callie about it," Misha said.

"When are you telling the boys?" Kyle asked.

"Tomorrow night, when Callie picks them up from day care."

Kyle smiled at him. "It'll be okay, Mish. The boys need to know who they are. Don't let them struggle with their powers on their own."

Misha nodded. Kyle was speaking from experience, having struggled with her powers and feeling like an outsider her whole life, until they discovered she was half realm-demon. He didn't want the boys to suffer like that. They needed to know they were part demon even if they didn't know what clan they came from.

He had said the same thing to Callie, but that didn't stop his concern. Callie was nervous that she didn't have all the answers for her sons. But did a parent ever have all the answers for their children? Everything would be okay for Callie and her boys.

Misha would make damn sure of it.

CHAPTER 9

The boys sat like two bookends on the lime green couch, gazing at Misha with wide eyes. Callie could understand their trepidation. Her nerves had been dancing along her spine since picking them up from day care after work. Her boys had always been intuitive, and when she drove them to the BSR office instead of home, they both knew something was up.

Callie perched between her sons and took a deep breath.

"We've been good, Momma. We haven't shown anyone our powers," Matty blurted before she could start her speech.

"I know you haven't, honey. You're not in trouble. I need to talk to you about why it's important to not show others your powers." She looked over at Misha, who signaled to her to continue. "You both realize that not everyone has powers, right?"

They nodded at the same time.

"So if others see what you can do, they will want to know how you can make things move with your mind or blow things up with a thought."

Luke frowned. "Hows come we do this?"

She rubbed her damp hands over her pants and decided now was not the time to correct his grammar.

"You're special. The reason you can do the things you do is because you are part demon."

The boys jerked upright in their seats.

Matty's lip trembled before he spoke. "Demons are monsters, Momma. They hurt people. Are we monsters?"

Callie's heart seized. Before she could force any words past her lips, Misha spoke.

"If demons are monsters, then I am a monster too," he said.

The boys gaped at him. "You're a demon like us?" Luke asked.

"Yes, I am. There are many other demons as well who live among humans. You are not alone."

The boys looked at each other for a moment. Callie wondered if they were somehow communicating. They had always seemed to communicate very well without words. In the past she chalked it up to them being identical twins, but now she wondered if it was part of their powers.

"Can all demons do what we do?" Luke asked.

Misha leaned forward in his chair. "Demons have different powers. Some can do what you do, and others can do other things."

"Momma, are you a demon?" Luke asked.

"No. But your father was."

"I don't want to be different from Momma," Matty whispered.

Callie leaned over and grabbed both her sons' hands. "You both have part of me inside you."

"You have your momma's eyes."

"But we're not human," Matty argued.

"You're half human and half demon," Callie answered.

"But we have to keep it a secret from our friends," Luke said, looking between Callie and Misha.

Misha nodded.

Matty swung his legs, his heels hitting the couch. "Because we scare normal people."

Callie blinked back a tear. She would not cry right now. She would not upset her sons any further than she already had.

"Yes," Misha replied when she didn't respond immediately. "Humans are afraid of what they don't understand."

"We'll never use our powers again," Luke blurted.

Misha shook his head. "That's not why we told you the truth. We want you to understand why you have powers, and learn who you can and can't show your powers to. You also need to learn how to control your powers so you don't accidentally hurt someone. Never using your powers again is not the answer. You need someone to show you how to use them correctly."

Callie squeezed the boys' hands. She and Misha had already discussed this. He had spoken to one of the clan elders, who agreed to train the boys in how to use their powers.

Luke sat up straighter. "Can you train us, Mr. Misha?"

Misha's ice blue eyes widened. "I actually had someone else in mind."

Matty blurted. "We want you."

"Boys—"

Misha held up his hand. "It's okay, Çallie. How about this? I'll work with you at first, and then we'll talk about having you work with one of my clan elders."

"Clan?" Matty looked at Callie. "Are demons Scottish like the stories you read us?"

Misha chuckled. "Do I sound Scottish to you?"

Matty shook his head. "No, you sound like that bad guy Boris in *Rocky and Bullwinkle*."

Misha's chuckle graduated to a laugh. "Have you been watching the classic cartoon network?"

The boys giggled. Callie was able to take her first deep breath of the night.

"My clan is originally from Russia, but demons come from all over the world."

"So where does our clan come from?" Matty asked.

Callie's throat tightened. So much for feeling relaxed. "I'm not sure what clan your father belonged to, honey."

"We're working on finding that out for you," Misha added. "In the meantime, you are both honorary members of my Shamat clan and will be trained at our compound."

Matty moved to the edge of the couch. "Do we have to learn Russian?"

Misha smiled. "Only if you want to. So let's agree. You will both not use your powers outside of our training sessions. We have a deal, yes?"

"Yes," both boys chimed in.

"Do you have any other questions for us right now?" Misha asked.

The boys looked at each other for a moment before blurting. "When do we start?"

———————————

Callie climbed into bed with a long sigh. She had finally gotten the boys fed and ready for bed. They had been bouncing off the walls after the discussion with Misha, peppering her with questions she couldn't answer about the training, but she was fine with that.

Better those questions than ones about their father. Those would come eventually, after the boys processed everything else. A lot of information had been thrown their way today, and they were handling it like troopers. Better than she was, truth be told. She was emotionally exhausted.

Her phone rang, and she suppressed a whimper. She should pull the covers over her head and ignore it.

She glanced at the screen. It was Misha. She made a grab for her cell to stop it from going to voicemail. "Hello."

"Hello, Callie, I hope I'm not interrupting anything."

"No. I finally got the boys in bed a few minutes ago."

"Good. I called to make sure they're doing okay."

"Surprisingly, yes. They can't wait to start their training. They asked me if they need some sort of uniform like karate, and I told them I had no idea."

Misha chuckled. "They're good boys. How are you doing with all this?"

"Okay. I know that they'll have more questions later, but they don't appear to be traumatized by our discussion, so that's a plus."

"Children are much more accepting of things than adults. They'll be good pupils."

Callie ran her hand along the comforter edge. "Thank you for agreeing to train them. You didn't have to do that."

"They are more comfortable with me, so it makes sense for me to train them at first."

"It was nice of you to tell them they are honorary members of your clan. Don't you have to ask permission before you do something like that? I don't want you to get in trouble."

"No trouble. I have an in with the clan leader, since he's my father. Plus, once he gets a look at your boys, he'll act like he came up with the idea himself."

Callie chuckled. "He sounds interesting."

"Just you wait. My babushka will grab hold of the boys and spoil them rotten."

"Babushka?"

"My grandmother. I'll tell the compound guards to grant you and the twins access to the compound for your training sessions. Your boys will be part of the clan in no time."

Callie blinked back tears. "Thank you."

"You're welcome."

Was it her imagination, or had his voice gotten deeper?

"Get a good night's sleep, Callie. You deserve it."

He disconnected, and she lay back against her pillow. It was hard to believe that a short time ago she was afraid of Misha. Thought his eyes were cold and his demeanor intimidating.

Now. Now she saw the wonderful man...male he was. Taking her sons under his wing and ensuring they would safely learn about their powers. Callie wasn't surprised her boys had grown fond of him in such a short time. She certainly had.

But she needed to put the brakes on her growing feelings for Misha. Having the boys become part of a clan was vital for their future, and she couldn't afford to screw things up for them by being attracted to someone who didn't see her in the same way.

This was about the boys, not her. And she would do absolutely anything to ensure their happiness.

CHAPTER 10

Callie checked her phone for the time as she hurried down the hall toward the immigration office. She was supposed to be there at eight a.m. sharp to start the conference call. Both Aleksei and Doyle were out in the field, and this was the first time Aleksei trusted her to run the vendor meeting. She couldn't let him down.

It had taken longer than normal to get the boys ready for day care this morning. They were still full of questions about what it meant to be a demon and when, when, when would they begin training with Mr. Misha?

Callie reached into her bag and pulled out her key ring. The key barely turned before the door opened and she rushed into the space. She typed in the alarm code and gasped as she stepped inside.

The main office was a mess. Paper and office items were strewn everywhere. Furniture lay in pieces on the floor. Something red splattered across the floor—was that blood?

Her heart tried to flee through her throat. What if whoever did this was still here? She clutched her key ring in her hand and backed up quietly toward the door.

Her purse banged into the doorjamb, and she jumped at the noise. So much for sneaking out.

She took another step and slammed into a hard stomach. Hands grabbed her shoulders, and she screamed.

———————

Misha grinned at the box of deliciousness perched in his lap. A dozen donuts from the bakery across from Kyle's apartment tempted him. He turned his smile on his teammate in the back seat of the van as Jean Luc drove.

"Kyle, you outdid yourself this time. What's the occasion?"

She shrugged. "I thought you could use some nourishment after meeting with the twins last night. How did it go?"

"Good. The boys actually took it well."

"And how did Callie do?" Jean Luc asked.

"Worried, but that's what a good mother does, yes?"

"*Oui.* Did you convince the twins not to use their powers in public?"

"Yes. We made a deal. They can use their powers, but only when they're training at the demon compound."

Jean Luc turned the corner. "Did you ask one of your elders to train them?"

"I did, but the plans have changed. I'm going to be training them."

Kyle laughed. "How did you get roped into that?"

"The boys asked me to, and I'm fine with helping them if it makes them more comfortable. I told Callie we would talk later today to schedule the time. She had a call first thing this morning at the office while Aleksei and Doyle are at the new halfway house with the contractor. Now if you two are done badgering me, I am going to enjoy my donuts."

Misha had only polished off donut number two when his phone buzzed. He looked at the screen and frowned.

"What is it, Mish?" Kyle asked.

"The alarm at the immigration office is going off. Callie is there alone. Jean Luc —"

"On our way there now. We are less than ten minutes away."

Kyle leaned forward. "Maybe Callie forgot to turn off the alarm."

Misha's stomach soured. "It's the panic button. You have to push it on purpose." He dialed Callie's number. The phone kept ringing. *Pick up, pick up!*

He swore in Russian. "She's not answering."

Jean Luc sped up.

Misha called the number again. By the third unanswered call, Jean Luc had pulled into the parking lot in front of the building, and before he could put the van in park, Misha was out the passenger door and running into the building, Kyle's footsteps pounding close behind him.

He ran down the hallway and flung open the door, looking through the trashed office until he saw Callie hovering over Aleksei, who sat on a chair with a towel over his eyes.

Misha grabbed Callie by the arms. "What happened? Are you okay?"

She looked up at him, her green eyes wide and frightened. "I'm fine. I came into the office and found this mess and as I was leaving..." She looked over at his brother who had pulled the towel of his face. His eyes and the skin around them were flame red.

"I...ah...pepper-sprayed Aleksei. I carry a canister on my keychain." She reached for a new towel from a bowl of water and handed it to Aleksei. "I can't tell you how sorry I am."

Aleksei took the new towel and wiped his red-rimmed eyes. "It was an accident. I'm glad you defended yourself, even if it was against me."

Doyle walked into the main room from the back offices and shook his head. "For once I'm glad I'm short. I was behind Aleksei when Callie attacked him."

Callie put her hands on her hips. "I didn't attack him."

"You slammed your purse into him and then sprayed him," Doyle said with barely suppressed glee.

"Neither of you were supposed to be here this morning. When I saw the damage, I thought you were the bad guys."

"Our appointment was postponed. How did you know something happened?" Aleksei asked Misha.

"The office panic button went off."

Doyle walked over to the alarm panel by the door. "Yep, it's tripped. Probably happened when Aleksei fell back against it after Callie attacked him."

"Would you stop saying that!" Callie's voice rose an octave.

Misha glanced to the alarm panel. "Callie, did you turn off the alarm when you came in this morning?"

"Yes. I typed in the code before I turned and saw the damage."

"So someone broke in here without disturbing the alarm."

"Wouldn't they need to know the code?" Callie asked.

Jean Luc stepped up beside Misha. He wasn't sure how long the vampire had been there, but he had caught up on what was happening. "Or a demon was able to short-circuit it with their powers."

Misha nodded. "We'll have to pull the video footage to see if we captured anything. I'm worried that if they were able to turn off the alarm, they probably sabotaged the video, too, but we'll double check."

"How do the back offices look?" Aleksei asked Doyle.

"Similar to the safe house. The bad news is, the computers are toast."

Aleksei stood even though Callie tried to get him to stay seated. "Losing the computers is going to put us behind on the next relocation."

Kyle punched at an imaginary person in front of her. "Damn it! We need to call an emergency Council meeting."

Aleksei held up his hand. "Let's think about this before we go to the Demon Council."

Kyle frowned. "We need to let them know what's going on."

"Excuse me—" Callie said.

"I don't think we need to alarm anyone yet," Aleksei responded.

"I disagree," Kyle argued.

"Hey!" Callie hollered.

Everyone turned to her, and Misha grinned at her spunk.

"We didn't lose our stuff."

"What do you mean?" Aleksei asked.

"I mean that I set up a cloud backup system for our computers a few days ago and backed up our files. We lost a day's worth of work at the most."

Misha was impressed.

Kyle apparently was as well since she did a little happy dance. "Oh, sister, I knew it was a good idea hiring you. I told Aleksei you were perfect for the job."

Aleksei swept Callie up into a hug. "You're an asset to this organization, Callie."

Misha barely managed to resist decking his brother. He had warned Aleksei about taking advantage of

Callie. But it was only a celebratory hug…a hug that was going on too damn long for his taste, especially when Callie's cheeks turned pink.

"Put me down, Aleksei. You're hurt."

He set her down. "I'll be fine in a few minutes. Demons bounce back faster than humans when it comes to injuries."

"I don't care. Sit down."

Shockingly, his brother actually listened to her. She dipped a towel in the water and gently wiped Aleksei's eyes again.

Misha clenched his fist. "I'm going to check out the video feed to see if we can figure out who broke in."

Misha stomped toward the door to grab a laptop from the van and Jean Luc fell in step beside him.

He looked over at Misha and arched his eyebrows. "All is well, *mon ami*. Callie is safe, and you can stop glaring now."

Was she safe? Misha looked over his shoulder at Callie still hovering over Aleksei. He would have to remind his brother again that she was off limits. If he didn't heed his warning, Aleksei's red-rimmed eyes would be black and blue by the time Misha was finished with him.

CHAPTER 11

Callie pulled up to the large metal gate of the Shamat compound. An intimidating man—or really intimidating male, since she imagined he was a demon—stepped out of the small building attached to the gate and leaned down as Callie rolled down her window.

"Welcome Ms. Roberts. We've been expecting you."

Callie gaped at him. "How—"

"Did I know it was you?" He smiled. "I was given a picture of you and told you would be arriving this morning. You're expected at the community center, which is straight ahead about a mile and then turn right at the stop sign. You won't be able to miss the building. To the right of the building you will find the door leading to immigration's temporary offices."

"Thank you," Callie said as the large gate slowly opened in front of her. She drove straight through and followed the directions the guard gave her, gaping at the surroundings. She hadn't known what to expect when Misha told her about the demon compound, but this was definitely not it. Beautiful landscaping and trees greeted her as she drove down the lane. To the left she could see homes lining a side street. Each was unique, yet there was something tying them together— maybe it was the coordinating colors of the houses, or the small trees gracing each curb lawn.

She stopped at the stop sign and looked to her right at the community center, a large building of white clapboard and stone with tall windows. She then drove around the side of the building and parked next to the side entrance. As she made her way toward the building with her box in hand, the glass door opened, and Misha came out to join her.

"Let me get that."

Before she could protest, he grabbed the box.

"Did you have any trouble getting here?" Misha asked.

"No. Your directions were perfect, and the guards knew to expect me."

"Let me show you around the space."

Callie followed Misha into the building and down the hall to the third door on the left. Misha held open the door for her with one hand as he held her box with the other as if it weighed nothing. The room he escorted her into was large, with two desks and a conference table with six chairs around it.

Misha set her box on the desk closest to the door and turned to her. "This room will be for you and Doyle." He pointed to a door on the right-hand wall. "That leads to another office for Aleksei. Across the hall is a copy room and the bathroom. Do you need me to help you carry in anything else from the car?"

"No. This is all I have right now. Aleksei and Doyle are following with the rest of our stuff."

Misha nodded. "The space should work until we're able to get the offices cleaned up."

"Were you able to get anything from the security videos?"

"Very little. There is a blurry outline of someone, and then the cameras cut out. But I have a computer program working on the resolution of the photograph we do have. We might still get lucky."

Callie started to unpack her box and set her supplies on her desk. The boys had been pestering her about when they could begin their training with Misha, but she hesitated to ask him since he was so busy with the case. Before she could get her nerve up, the door opened and Aleksei and Doyle walked inside.

Aleksei grinned. "Good to see you made it, Callie. Brother, we could use your help bringing in the supplies."

Misha walked out the door with Aleksei. Callie turned and found Doyle studying her closely.

"What's wrong?" she asked.

"I've seen that look before."

Something fluttered in Callie's stomach. "What look?"

"You've got a thing for the big Russian."

"Don't be silly. Misha and I are just friends."

Doyle chuckled. "I didn't say which Russian I was talking about. It's interesting that you assumed I meant Misha."

Callie's cheeks heated, and she stopped herself from patting them. Doyle's chuckle turned into a laugh.

"Shouldn't you be outside helping them bring in the supplies?"

Doyle shrugged. "They'll be fine. I'd much rather continue our conversation."

"We aren't having a conversation."

"Funny, but when two people talk with each other, isn't it called a conversation?" Doyle's eyebrows rose.

"Let me rephrase. We aren't having *this* conversation."

"You're no fun," he grumbled. "I'm only trying to get to know my coworker better."

"Are you actually pouting?" Callie laughed.

"What's so funny?" Aleksei asked as he walked through the door carrying three boxes stacked one on top of the other.

Misha followed behind him with his own stack of boxes, setting them down on the floor next to Aleksei's. "Yes, what did we miss?"

Callie looked frantically over at Doyle, praying he wouldn't say anything, but the smirk on his face made her stomach bottom out.

"Callie asked me if I was going to come help you with the boxes, but I figured you two manly demons would handle it, and I was right."

Misha sighed. "Trust you to try to get out of work, Doyle."

Doyle smiled. "Some of us were made for management. Others were made for manual labor."

Callie couldn't stop the laugh from escaping. "All right, you guys, it's time to get this office into shape. The boxes with the letter "A" on the top need to go into Aleksei's office. The other boxes need to stay in this room. Let's set the boxes on the conference table, and we can get organized. The sooner we finish, the sooner we're back in business."

The three men stared at her with wide eyes.

"Why do you look so surprised? Some of us were made for management."

Misha's eyes danced. His chuckle quickly turned into a deep belly laugh. Callie had never heard him laugh like that before. It was a wonderful sound, and it made her heart speed up to know she had caused it. She pulled her gaze away from him and concentrated on the box in front of her. It was time to get back to work.

An hour later Callie was finally settled at her desk and working. It hadn't taken long to get her desk in order. Misha had left to go back to the BSR, and Doyle followed him out soon after to check on the status of the new halfway house. Aleksei was in his own office on a conference call. Finally, some peace and quiet.

Callie was a patient woman for the most part. She had to be with twin boys, but being surrounded by demon males tested her patience.

She'd just started reviewing their schedule for the week when the office door opened and a large male strode into the room. He was dressed in a very expensive suit and looked enough like Aleksei to be his older brother. Except the eyes. His eyes were ice blue, exactly like Misha's.

"May I help you?"

"You must be Callie. I'm Boris."

Callie stood. Misha and Aleksei's father—that explained everything. "It's so good to meet you, sir."

"None of this 'sir' business. You must call me Boris. I've heard a lot about you from my son. He is very impressed."

Which son was he talking about? But Callie knew better than to ask. She learned that lesson with Doyle this morning.

"Thank you for letting us set up our offices here temporarily."

Boris waved his hand. "Not a problem. We need to keep this immigration plan going. We won't let a bunch of vandal cowards stop us." He flashed a brilliant smile. "If there is anything I can do to help you get settled in, please let me know."

Callie couldn't help but smile back at him. He was one smooth customer.

"Aleksei asked me to stop by this morning. Is he available?"

Callie looked down at the phone on her desk. The light next to Aleksei's line was no longer red. "It looks like Aleksei has finished his conference call. I'll let him know you're here."

She walked over to his door and tapped lightly on it.

"Enter."

She opened the door and leaned inside. "Your father is here to see you."

Aleksei checked his watch. "That's a record for him. He actually waited an hour before he came over here."

"I heard that," Boris called from the outer office.

Aleksei got to his feet. "I apologize for not warning you he was coming."

"I heard that, too."

"Welcome to my life," Aleksei whispered.

Callie giggled. She knew without a doubt that this job would never be boring.

Boris stood in the doorway. "Did you not ask me to come over here so we could discuss the next Council meeting?"

"I mentioned that we need to get together, yes. I didn't expect you to show up this morning."

"But I'm here now, yes? So let us talk."

"Do you need me to stay and take notes?" Callie asked.

"Actually, I think that's a great idea," Aleksei replied. "Why don't we have our conversation at the conference table?"

They walked back into the main office. Callie grabbed her new laptop and settled at the conference table. Thirty minutes into the conversation, Callie came to two conclusions. The first was that Aleksei and Boris butted heads. And second, they butted heads because they were so much alike. Boris was a bit more of a showman, a true politician, where Aleksei was more straightforward. But they were both stubborn and used to getting their way.

Aleksei wanted to meet with all the Council members and demand their cooperation in helping to stop the protests. Boris felt a more diplomatic approach was needed.

"Father, I understand that you're trying to keep peace with the Council. But if we don't convince them to step up now, it's going to get even harder as more realm demons come to earth. The other clans might not listen to you or me, but they may listen to their own clan leaders. And don't forget, Kyle is the spokesperson for this project and will be at the Council meeting."

"Ah, yes. And your sister does not have a diplomatic bone in her body."

Callie set up straighter. "Kyle is your and Misha's sister?"

Aleksei grinned. "She's not related by blood. Misha proclaimed her our *sestra* after Kyle saved his life. Although if you listen to the way she talks to me, you would think we were related. She is exactly what I would imagine an annoying younger sister would be like."

Boris chuckled. "And now Misha has requested that your sons be made honorary clan members."

Callie bit nervously at her lip. "I hope that's okay?"

"Of course, of course. We are happy to help guide your sons in the use of their powers. Misha has told me how great they are."

The door swung open and Kyle walked in.

"Speak of the devil, and she shall appear," Aleksei said.

Boris stood, rounded the table, and took Kyle in his arms. "It is good to see you, my daughter."

Kyle chuckled after he released her. "I don't know what I'm going to do with you, Boris." She looked at Callie. "Are you having a fun time with these two?"

"So far," she said.

Kyle sat down next to Callie at the conference table and looked at Callie's computer screen. "Just as I thought. Talking about the next Council meeting. I figured I'd better be here to referee while you argue about the best way to handle the situation."

Boris sat in his spot again as well. "We are not arguing, Kyle. We are discussing the options."

Kyle looked at Callie again. "Have they been having a discussion or an argument?"

Callie looked between the two males. "Ahhhh, I would say they've been having a passionate disagreement."

Kyle rested her head in her hands. "Oh, no. You've spent an hour with Boris, and he's already turning you to the dark side."

Boris laughed. A deep belly laugh that reminded Callie of Misha. "You are right, Aleksei, Callie is impressive."

So it had been Aleksei who told Boris she was impressive. She shouldn't be surprised, really. Misha was taken with her sons, and that was a good thing. The boys needed a strong male influence in their lives. She was thankful, and it was selfish on her part to hope for more.

"Yes, she is, which is why I told Aleksei to hire her." Kyle preened. "Before we decide what we should say to the Council, I think we should meet with Naya. We should find out how things are going in the realm, since it's something the Council is sure to ask about."

Naya. Callie sat up straighter.

"Let's schedule a meeting." Kyle pulled a necklace out from under her T-shirt and began rubbing her fingers over what looked like some sort of crystal. "I'll contact her to find out when she can meet with us."

Callie stopped typing and Kyle caught her staring at the necklace. "Naya is telepathic. She gave me this crystal from the realm. It acts kind of like a conductor of telepathic energy."

Callie blinked. "I don't even know what to say about that."

"Sorry to throw yet another thing at you. You have to be on overload at this point."

Aleksei steered them back to the conversation. "We'll meet with Naya, but she is not going to tell us what to do."

Kyle smiled. "Whatever do you mean?"

"You know exactly what I mean. Whenever we meet with her, she disagrees with everything we suggest."

"Naya is not used to having to discuss her decisions. Living in the realm means making split-second decisions to keep herself and others alive."

"Which is well and good, but she doesn't understand how things work here. She's also stubborn and egotistical."

"Hmm." Kyle tapped her fingers against her chin. "Sounds like somebody I already know."

Boris coughed into his hand, and if Callie didn't know better, she would say he was hiding a laugh.

Aleksei ignored Kyle's comment. "See how soon Naya can meet with us, Kyle. We should know exactly what we're going to say to the Council before we meet with them, including what Naya will say."

Callie looked at the blinking cursor on her computer screen. She hadn't typed anything for several minutes. Not that she thought she needed to record Aleksei and Kyle's bickering. She typed one word on the screen.

Naya

She was finally going to meet the female Misha had a crush on. Was she ready?

CHAPTER 12

Misha glared at the fuzzy picture on his computer screen. The program he ran had improved the picture somewhat, but he still couldn't get a clear ID on the person who broke into the immigration office. Then he turned to the second laptop and scowled again. They had nothing on a Mark Stewart. He was striking out on both fronts.

"Why are you frowning so hard, big guy?" Kyle asked as she walked into the room.

"We need a break on one of these cases."

Kyle sat next to him and looked at the picture on the first computer screen. "Have we heard anything from Jean Luc and Jason?"

"They have not had any luck interviewing the neighbors around the vandalized halfway house again, or the other offices in the immigration building. Either no one saw anything, or they're afraid to tell the truth."

"And the twins' father?"

Misha snorted. "Mark Stewart is a ghost. I've not found anyone by that name who could be the twins' father in any of our databases, human or supernatural."

"Maybe Talia will find out something from her bounty contacts. Don't lose hope. The twins are in a much better position than I was at their age."

"I'm sorry, Kyle. I wish I had done something for you and your mother all those years ago. Maybe—"

Kyle rested her hand over his clenched fist. "Don't go there, Mish. You helped deliver me, but it doesn't mean you were responsible for my life."

Anger surged under Misha's skin. "Of course I'm responsible for you. I would die to protect you."

Kyle smiled at him. "And I would die for you as well. For years, it was you, Jean Luc, and me against the world. Now Talia, Jason, Sabrina, and Dalton have also become part of my family. A family that is so much more important to me because I chose them." She shook her head. "Enough of this. I'm getting mushy, and you know how much I hate being mushy."

"Yes, little one. I'm well aware. How did discussions go with Aleksei this morning?"

"You mean Aleksei and your father?"

Misha groaned. "I'm not surprised my father showed up to the offices first thing. I should have warned Callie."

Kyle chuckled. "She was having no trouble holding her own."

"I can imagine."

"We decided that we should meet with Naya before the next Council meeting. We want to find out if the trouble in the realm is escalating."

Right. Because trouble in the realm would not mean graffiti and broken office furniture, but rather life and death.

"She would have reached out to us if she was in trouble, would she not?"

"Maybe. Naya is used to taking care of herself."

Misha did not like to hear that. Of course he was happy that she was a strong, independent female. But he also wanted to ensure her safety. Kyle would call him an overprotective caveman, but he couldn't help wanting to protect Naya...and Callie, for that matter. He shuddered when he thought about what could have happened to Callie if she had walked into the immigration office while it was being vandalized.

A plan had been forming in his mind, and he would need Kyle's help to bring it to fruition. Even if she called him a caveman—or her favorite phrase, Neanderthal—it was worth it to keep Callie and the boys safe.

"I need your help with something."

The corners of Kyle's mouth quirked up into a grin. "You're giving me that look, Misha. The one you use when you want me to bring you pastries. It must be pretty important if you're willing to bat your baby blues at me."

"Very important. And I need your expertise to pull it off."

"Wow, now you're flattering me. I think you just channeled your father. You have my attention, so spill."

Misha began to lay out his plan.

The boys stood in the middle of the room, eyes wide as they took in the vast space. Callie wasn't surprised they were overwhelmed. She was overwhelmed. She felt like she was in an elite gym. Pristine exercise equipment lined the mirrored walls. Blue mats covered the floor where Misha directed the boys to stand. Callie hovered in the corner after promising Misha she wouldn't interfere with the training.

The boys looked over at her, and she gave them a thumbs-up and a smile, even though butterflies were taking flight in her stomach.

Misha walked out to the center of the mats and set a red plastic kick ball on the floor before squatting down in front of the boys.

"Before I can train you, I need to understand the extent of your powers. Luke, I'm going to start with you. You are able to move things with your mind, yes?"

Luke nodded.

"Let us start with something simple. I would like you to move the ball. Simply roll it toward us."

Luke gaped at him. "You want me to use my power?"

"Yes. As we discussed, you can't use your powers outside the compound, but when you're here, you can practice your powers under supervision."

Luke stared at the ball until it started to vibrate. After a few moments, the ball rolled toward them.

"Very good, Luke. Can you raise it?"

Luke pursed his lips, the ball lifted into the air a few inches.

"Excellent. Can you raise it even higher?"

The ball hovered in the same spot before shooting across the room and bouncing off the mirrored wall. Luke stomped his foot and looked down at the floor.

"No worries, Luke. You did a great job. With some training you'll be able to better control your powers. Matty? What about you?"

"I can't pick things up like that."

Luke chimed in. "He only blows things up."

Matty glared at his brother. "I don't mean to blow things up."

"Of course you don't," Misha said. He walked over to a box against the wall and pulled out a small pillow. He set the pillow in the spot where the ball had been.

"Explain to me what happens, Matty, when things blow up, like your birthday cake."

Matty sighed. "Umm… I think about the cake, and I can see its insides."

"What do you mean by insides?"

"The cake started to sparkle, and I could see through it. Then the sparkles started to spin, and that's when the cake blew up."

Callie's flittering butterflies had turned into dive bombers at her son's description. She'd spent the last year telling her sons not to use their powers. Maybe she should have tried to understand them instead. But she wouldn't have known how to teach them to use or control their powers.

"Okay, I want you to concentrate on the pillow."

Matty nodded and clenched his hands into fists as he stared at the pillow.

"Can you see the sparkles?"

"Yes."

"Make the sparkles move."

The pillow shot up into the air and burst apart, feathers shooting across the mat. Callie clapped her hand over her mouth to stop the gasp, but Matty still saw her reaction.

"I'm sorry, Momma."

"There's nothing to be sorry about, baby."

"She's right," Misha said.

"What good is my power?"

"We'll figure that out together. If both of you want to continue with your training, that is."

Luke nodded enthusiastically while Matty shrugged.

Misha squatted down in front of the boys again. "What's wrong, Matty?"

Matty scraped his foot along the mat. "What if you can't train me?"

"Enough of that negativity, Matty Roberts."

The boys spun at the voice. "Kyle!" they both hollered.

"Hello, my little friends. I think I arrived right on time to stop the grumbling."

The boys looked at each other for a moment, then shrugged.

Callie took a step toward the boys, but Misha shook his head slightly at her.

Kyle walked over and stood between the twins. "Tell me what you're worried about."

Matty bit his lip and looked away.

Kyle crossed her arms. "Let me guess. You feel scared. Like you wonder if you'll ever understand your powers, or if you'll ever fit in with your human friends and any demon friends you make."

Luke's eyes widened as Matty answered. "Yes. How did you know?"

"Because I felt the same way when I found out I was half demon."

Callie's hand went over her mouth again to stop the new gasp from emerging. She didn't want to interrupt the conversation. Both boys stepped closer to Kyle, and she sat cross-legged on the floor and beckoned for the boys to sit next to her on the mat.

Once they were seated she looked at both of them. "I used to worry about a lot of things. I spent my whole life not understanding why I could change people's memories. Now I understand that I'm not alone anymore. You two are lucky, because you've always had each other and your Mom to look out for you. Now you also have me, and Misha, and a whole clan to look out for you and help you along the way."

Callie blinked back tears as the boys looked over at her, grinning. She didn't know how she was ever going to repay Kyle and Misha for everything they were doing for her sons. She wasn't used to others watching her back. It was definitely a feeling she could get used to.

Kyle and the boys started playing when Misha walked over to her. "Callie, I want to talk to you about something."

She looked up into his eyes. Determined eyes. He was up to something.

"Did you practice whatever speech you're about to say?"

His eyes lost their seriousness as a grin brightened his face. "How did you know?"

"You have the same look you had the day at the food trucks, when you tried to talk me into telling the twins the truth."

"And it worked. You did."

She chuckled. "I told you I already had decided to do it."

Misha shrugged. "Maybe, maybe not."

"So what are you going to try and convince me to do this time?"

"Will you walk with me?"

Callie looked back at the boys. They were spinning in circles on the mats and laughing when they fell on their bums.

"They'll be fine. Kyle is going to watch over them."

"Is she in on this too?"

"Maybe."

Callie held her hand out. "Lead the way."

Misha led her out of the building and walked slowly down the sidewalk with her next to him.

"What do you think of the clan compound so far?"

"Honestly? I'm impressed. I didn't know what to expect, but it wasn't this. It's like a small suburban community."

"Yes, my father and the elders wanted to create a place where our clan feels safe. We have over a hundred homes, the community center, and a small hospital, and I've been thinking. Now that the boys know what they are, it might make sense for you to stay here for a while. They could play with other children like them and learn to control their powers without exposure to humans."

Callie stopped. "Are you saying we need to hide them away?"

"Of course not. Not everyone in our clan lives here. They come and go at will. The purpose of this compound is not to hide. It's to build community."

Callie looked at the beautiful homes lining the streets. "I couldn't afford to live here, Misha."

"Yes, you could. We have empty houses available for rent. I know of the perfect place for the boys. It even has a swing set in the backyard."

"This is a big step."

"When is your contract up on your rental house?"

"It's already up."

Misha turned to her. "Are you going to renew it?"

"I haven't decided yet. My landlord gave me a three-month extension to let me decide, and that ends in two weeks."

His eyes narrowed. "You aren't planning on leaving, are you?"

She squirmed under his penetrating gaze. "I was. Before."

"Now?"

"Now I think it makes sense to let the boys spend time with your clan to learn how to control their powers."

"I agree. Which is why you should move here. Did I mention we have a grade school, too?"

She opened her mouth and he held up his hand. "Don't say no until you see the house." They walked one more block, and Callie gaped at the wonderful homes on either side of the picturesque street. Misha stopped in front of a gray ranch house with a pretty front yard.

Callie fell in love with it before they stepped inside. But she wasn't about to let Misha know that yet. He unlocked the door and the entryway led into an open floor plan with a living room straight ahead and a kitchen to the left. A breakfast room with a view of the backyard perched in between. A fenced-in backyard — she stumbled over to the window and gaped — with a play set that included a jungle gym, swings, small rock wall, and circular slide.

"That is amazing!"

Misha chuckled next to her. "Isn't it? The minute I saw it, I knew the twins would go bonkers."

"Where did the family go who lived here before?"

"They moved to Russia for a year. It's kismet. The house is furnished and has three bedrooms, an office, and two bathrooms."

Two bathrooms. Callie couldn't remember when she had ever had an uninterrupted moment in the bathroom. Since the twins were born, the answer was never. This seemed too perfect.

"Does your wanting us to live here have to do with the break-in at the office?"

Misha frowned and glanced away for a moment. "I won't lie and say it didn't play a part in my suggesting this. But I think it makes sense for the boys to be here right now, and it will be safer for you as well."

"I'm not quitting my job."

His eyes flashed. "I didn't ask you to."

"I would need to know the rent and review the contract."

"Of course. Would you like to see the rest of the house?"

They walked through the house, and Callie knew before they got to the master bedroom that she wanted it. The bungalow they lived in now had come furnished. So it would only be a matter of moving their clothes, bedding, bathroom and kitchen supplies. Since they moved so frequently, the fewer possessions they had, the better.

"Should we show the boys?" Misha asked.

She pursed her lips. "Now you're playing dirty. If the boys see this place, there will be no negotiating with them. We'll be here tomorrow."

"Then let's go get them."

Callie laughed. "You are a stubborn demon, Misha."

"That's what my babushka tells me as well."

"Thank you for everything." Callie cleared her throat. "I don't know if I can ever repay you and Kyle for what you've done for the boys."

His eyes tightened on her. "You don't need to repay us for anything, Callie. That's what friends do."

She stopped herself from cringing. If all he could offer her was friendship, she'd take it. Her brain accepted it...even while her heart protested.

"Did I mention my cousins own a moving company?"

She rolled her eyes. "Of course they do."

"So do we have a deal?"

"I don't have much choice, do I? Especially after you and the twins gang up on me."

Misha's eyes twinkled, much like the twins when they were up to something. "Very true. Now, can we go get the boys to show them the house?"

"Fine. Lead the way, Misha, lead the way."

CHAPTER 13

Misha watched Luke and Matty try to lug boxes into their new home.

Callie hadn't exaggerated about the twins' enthusiasm once they saw the house. They were moving in two days after their initial conversation.

It didn't hurt that his cousins owned a moving company and were able to fit the move into their schedules. His cousins literally had the van loaded, transported, and unloaded in less than two hours with the items Callie needed moved. The fact that Callie had very little she could call her own troubled him. Probably in her mind it made moving easier. In his mind it meant she didn't have a sense of permanence.

Misha held open the door with his foot as the boys staggered inside and dropped their box on the floor. Luckily it was full of unbreakable items.

"Why don't you guys go unpack the boxes in your room while I help your mom?"

Even though the boys could each have had their own bedroom, they chose to share one. Misha made sure they were in their room staying out of trouble before he went down the hall to the master bedroom. He found Callie unloading bedding from a box.

Misha set the box he was carrying next to the door. "That should be the last of the boxes from outside. What do you need help with?"

"You've already done enough already. It won't take me long to get everything organized."

"You've got me for at least the next hour, until Kyle shows up with dinner for everyone." He held up his hand before she could protest. "No arguing about dinner. The last thing you're going to want to do after unpacking is make dinner. You still need to go grocery shopping to restock anyway."

"Fine," she replied...rather grudgingly Misha thought...but it was a victory nonetheless.

"Let me help you with the bed."

She nodded as she dropped the fitted sheet on the bed. "I would say that I can do it, but it's a king, and it would probably take me an hour to make myself. I've never had such a big bed."

"Actually, it's a California king," Misha announced as he tucked the corner.

"How do you know for sure?"

Crap. "Because I have one myself. Shamat males tend to take up a lot of space."

"Obviously." Callie's eyes got huge when she realized what she'd said, and she grabbed a pillowcase, spending an inordinate amount of time putting it on the pillow and fluffing it afterward.

Misha helped her pull the new blankets up on the bed.

When Callie stood, parts of her blond hair came out of the ponytail. She tucked the loose strands behind her ear, and Misha took in her flushed face and sparkling green eyes.

"There are extra blankets in the chest at the end of the bed."

"How did you know that?"

Where the hell had his brain gone?

"Hello? Is anyone home?"

Misha never thought his Babushka's habit of showing up uninvited would save the day.

Callie looked up at him with wide eyes. "The van just left, so who could be showing up already?"

"I have a pretty good idea. You are about to meet the real boss of this compound. And if you ever tell my father I said that, I'll deny it."

He held out his hand, and Callie hesitated for a moment before grasping. He pulled her lightly down the hall to the living room. His babushka stood in the entryway with a dish in her hand.

"Babushka this is Callie. Callie, this is Irina Chesnokov, my grandmother."

Babushka beamed at Callie. "It is so good to finally meet you. I wanted to welcome you to the compound."

"So nice to meet you, ma'am."

"None of that ma'am business. Please call me Irina." Babushka looked around the room. "Everything looks great already. I was hoping to meet your boys. I hear they're delightful."

"They're in their room. Let me go get them."

Callie went to get the boys, and Misha turned to Irina. "This may be a new record for you, Babushka. The moving van left less than five minutes ago."

She waved her hand. "You're exaggerating. Anton texted me when they left, and that was at least ten minutes ago."

Misha chuckled. "I stand corrected."

Before Babushka could reprimand him for his cheeky response—and by the look in her eyes he would have gotten an earful—Callie came back in the living room with the boys following her.

Callie put her hand on each boy's head as she introduced them. "Matty, Luke, this is Misha's grandmother, Miss Irina."

Babushka grinned. "I'm so happy to meet you two. Mikhail has told me so much about you."

"Who is Mikhail?" Luke asked.

"I am," Misha answered. "Just like Matty's name is short for Matthew, Misha is short for Mikhail."

"Exactly. I was the one who got to choose Mikhail's name when he was born, but he insists on everyone calling him Misha." She sighed dramatically. "Such a beautiful name, and he refuses to use it. So I call him Mikhail."

The twins giggled.

"I brought some cookies I made this morning. I thought you might need to build your strength back up after working so hard moving today."

Matty and Luke stood on their tiptoes to peek over the top of the plate. It was Babushka's turn to giggle. "If it is okay with your mom, you can take the plate into the kitchen and each have one cookie."

The boys turned expectantly toward Callie.

"That would be fine. But only one. Kyle is bringing us dinner."

Babushka handed Luke the plate. "If you want to have more than one later, I would find a good place to hide the cookies from Mikhail. He is the original cookie monster."

The boys galloped straight to the kitchen.

Babushka turned back to Callie. "So what do you think of the house?"

"We love it." Callie smiled. "I can't believe how lucky we were that one of your families went to Russia for a year."

Misha's stomach bottomed out as he saw the look of confusion on Irina's face. He took a step closer to his grandmother. "Yes, I was telling Callie this was fate. They needed a place to stay, and we had an open house in the compound. The twins can continue their training, and with Callie working in the temporary immigration offices here, the location is perfect."

Irina beamed. "I agree. It's perfect for everyone concerned."

Misha let out the breath he'd been holding.

"Callie, I don't want to keep you from your unpacking. Do you mind if I borrow Mikhail for a few minutes and have him escort me home?"

Misha opened his mouth to protest, but Callie interrupted him before he could get the words out.

"Of course. We'll be fine. Misha, take your time."

Misha opened the front door and escorted his grandmother out to the sidewalk. They'd only taken a few steps before his grandmother turned to him and planted her hands on her hips.

"You're going to explain to me, dear grandson, why that wonderful woman thinks a family lived in that house."

Misha sighed. "Because if I told her the truth, she would never have moved here. She prides herself on being independent. She's never had anybody she can rely on."

"Your heart is in the right place. However, I think you may be asking for trouble. What do you think she'll do when she finds out this house belongs to you?"

"Hopefully by the time she figures that out, she'll be settled in here and won't want to move."

She sighed. "How in the world did you get that amusement park built in the back yard so quickly?"

Misha chuckled. "It's not an amusement park, Babushka. It's a next-generation jungle gym play set. I called in a few favors. Uncle Nikolai had a couple of his construction workers put it together. It only took them a day."

Irina pursed her lips before continuing. "Your father built you this house in the hopes that you would move back to the compound instead of continuing to live in your apartment."

"And I stay here on occasion, and eventually I'll move back to the compound permanently. But Callie and the boys need it more. They need the clan. And as much as I admire Callie for raising those boys on her own, they need our help."

"Luke and Matty are adorable. Of course they're welcome in the clan, as is Callie. This is a wonderful thing you're doing." She patted him on the arm. "I only hope it doesn't come back to bite you in the ass."

Leave it to Babushka not to pull any punches. And he hoped she was right as well. The last thing he wanted to do was alienate Callie. The more time he spent with her and the boys, the more he enjoyed having them around.

CHAPTER 14

Callie walked into the kitchen to check on the boys. She found them hunkered down, peeking into the cabinet under the sink.

"What are you two doing?"

Luke slammed the cabinet door shut. "Nothing!"

Both Matty and he stood up at the same time, trying—and failing miserably—to look innocent.

"Boys…"

Matty sighed. "We're doing what Miss Irina told us to do, hiding the cookies from Misha."

"The cookies are that good, huh?"

Luke nodded. "He's so big that we think if we put it down low he won't find it."

"Great idea, guys. Do you think you can help me straighten up the kitchen before Kyle comes with dinner?"

"Yes Momma," they chorused.

Callie had already wiped down the cabinets and countertops, so she was ready to put away the things cluttering up the table. She directed the boys where to put various pots and pans in the lower cabinets while she loaded the plates and glasses in the upper cabinets. Callie was wiping down the now-empty table when a knock sounded at the door.

"Kyle!" the boys hollered before running toward the front of the house.

"Slow down," she yelled as she followed them down the hall, but she was too late to stop them from opening the door. Even though they were in a gated community now, she still needed to remind them about not opening the door.

Kyle held up two plastic bags. "Hello, you two. Have you worked up an appetite moving in?"

"Yes," Matty said while Luke tried to peek into the bags.

Kyle chuckled. "I'll show you what's in the bag in a minute, silly boys. Jason will be here in a second with the rest of dinner. He's parking the car, and Jean Luc and Talia shouldn't be far behind."

Callie bit back a groan. She had never met Jason or Talia before, and now they were going to see her looking like a dirty mess.

Kyle watched her closely for a second before grimacing. "Misha didn't tell you we were all coming over, did he?"

"Um, no. He said you were coming. I'm not really set up to entertain yet."

"We're not expecting you to entertain us. We just thought it would be easier if you don't have to worry about dinner tonight."

"Thank you. I appreciate everything you guys have done for us."

Before Kyle could respond, a man walked up to the door. He looked to be in his thirties, with dark hair a little on the shaggy side.

"Callie, this is Jason, one of my teammates. Jason, meet Callie and her sons Matty and Luke."

Jason grinned at the boys. "I've heard a lot about you."

Callie beckoned for them to follow her to the kitchen. "Let's set the food down. I'll get some plates."

Kyle and Jason set the bags on the counter. "No worries on the plates and forks. I had the restaurant give us paper plates. I can't imagine you'd want to wash dishes tonight."

"Where's Misha?" Jason asked.

"He's walking his grandmother home. She came over to welcome us."

Kyle smirked. "I'll bet she did. Irina is one amazing lady. Not much goes on here that she doesn't know about."

Matty chimed in. "Miss Irina brought us cookies, but we had to hide them from Misha."

Jason laughed. "Smart thinking."

Kyle pulled out plates and plasticware and handed it to the boys. "Why don't you take the plates to the back patio table, and we'll have dinner there...if it's okay with your mom?"

Callie frowned. "I don't remember there being a back patio table when I looked at the house."

Kyle's eyes widened. "Really? Ahhh..."

"You wouldn't have seen it," Jason said. "Misha and I stopped over here earlier today to make sure everything was ready before the move, and we found the patio table folded up in the garage storage room. So we pulled it out and put it in the back for you and the boys. I mentioned it to Kyle on the way over here."

Before Callie could say thank you, Kyle grabbed the bags and carried them out the back French doors with the boys. Callie walked outside with Jason, and they sat and started passing around the food.

"Don't we need more plates?" Callie asked.

Kyle shook her head. "Nope. Jean Luc and Talia won't be eating with us."

"Why not?" Luke asked.

Probably because they were vampires, but the boys hadn't been told about other supernaturals yet. Callie had wanted to avoid overwhelming them, since they just found out they were demons. But the boys would need to learn about other paranormals as well.

Kyle gave her a quick look and then answered. "They already ate but still want to stop by to say hi."

Callie looked at the number of containers on the table. "Who is going to eat all this food?"

Kyle winked at the boys. "Who do you think?"

"Misha!" the boys yelled.

"Did I hear someone yell my name?" Misha asked as he joined the group on the patio. He took a look at the containers and his eyes danced. "Oh, Kyle, you brought Antonio's." He grinned at Callie. "You are in for a real treat. It's some of the best Italian food in the city."

Kyle nodded. "Yep, Antonio's is an Italian restaurant in my neighborhood. Tony packed something especially for the boys, too. Let's see if he got it right. I have spaghetti and meatballs."

"My favorite!" Luke said.

"And cheese ravioli."

"How did he know I love cheese ravioli?" Matty said, eyes big.

Kyle chuckled. "Tony never gets it wrong. He also sent food for the grownups."

Kyle filled the plates and handed them out to everyone, and Callie moaned out loud when she took a bite of the lasagna.

"That's how you're supposed to enjoy good food." Misha chuckled as he plopped another piece of garlic bread on his already full plate.

They ate in silence for a while. The twins both cleaned their plates before asking if they could be excused to play on their play set on steroids.

Kyle groaned as she watched them. "I don't know how they can play like that right after they finished eating."

Callie stood and picked up the empty containers. "Their settings are stuck on full tilt pretty much all the time."

"Do you need help?" Misha asked.

"No, you guys stay out here and watch the boys while I clean up."

Callie went inside and pulled out a small garbage bag, throwing away the empty containers and paper plates. A moment later Kyle carried in a handful of items as well.

"I know you said you can do this on your own, but you don't have to. And since I don't take direction very well, here I am."

Callie laughed. "I'll keep that under advisement."

"Seriously, I know what it's like to not want to rely on anybody, but I can promise you we're not going to go anywhere. You're stuck with the group of us."

Callie watched Matty and Luke as they clambered up the rock wall. Misha and Jason stood behind the boys making sure they were okay.

"Do you mind if I ask you something?"

"Shoot."

"Aleksei mentioned that you're an honorary member of the clan because you saved Misha's life. Can I ask what happened?"

Kyle leaned against the kitchen counter. "We were working a case, and Misha was shot protecting me. The bullet hit Misha in the shoulder, which normally wouldn't have been life-threatening for a demon, except the bullet was poisoned."

"Oh, my God," Callie exclaimed.

"Yeah, that was my reaction. I ended up having to pull the bullet out of his shoulder. After that he proclaimed me his *sestra* or sister, and I became a member of this clan."

"Please tell me you caught the guy who did it."

"Well... You could say that. Actually, it was Jason."

Callie looked out the window again. Jason and Misha were laughing at the boys' antics.

"What!"

"Jason isn't a bad guy. He thought all supernaturals were evil, and that Misha was going to hurt him. Misha ended up saving Jason's life, and then convinced him to work with us."

"Wow."

"It is quite a story. Misha has a very, very big heart. If it wasn't for him and Jean Luc, I don't know where I would be now."

Misha was wonderful. But she had to remind herself that helping people was part of Misha's nature, and she shouldn't read too much into him helping her. They were nothing more than friends.

The doorbell rang again, and Kyle volunteered to answer it. Callie took a deep breath and finished cleaning up while Kyle walked in with Jean Luc and a beautiful woman who was carrying plastic grocery bags. So this was Talia — vampire, supernatural bounty hunter, and Jean Luc's mate.

"Callie this is Talia. Talia, Callie."

Talia smiled at her. "It's nice to finally meet you. I can't believe how settled the house looks already."

"It doesn't take me long to get settled. I've moved a number of times."

Talia studied her a little too closely. "I know what it's like to travel light. Jean Luc and I decided to stop by for a moment so I can meet you. And I've heard so much about the boys. Do you mind if I say hi to them before we leave you to get settled?"

"Not at all. What's in the bags?" Callie asked.

"Jean Luc and I stopped at the store and bought a few staples for you until you can go grocery shopping."

Callie's stomach twisted. "You didn't have to do that."

"I know this is going to sound silly, but I loved it. I don't get to go food shopping for myself anymore, so it was a treat to pick out a few things for you. I got you some eggs, bread, milk, juice, and some lunchmeat."

"Tell me how much I owe you."

"That is not necessary," Jean Luc said.

Callie gritted her teeth before answering. "It is very necessary."

Jean Luc opened his mouth to speak again, but Talia set her hand on his arm. "No problem. It was around fifteen dollars."

Callie nodded. "If you'll excuse me for a minute, I'll go grab my purse."

"Sure," Kyle answered. "We'll go out back, and I'll introduce Talia to the boys."

Callie marched into her bedroom and reached for her purse, her hands shaking slightly. She sat down for a moment on the bed and shut her eyes.

"Callie, is something wrong?"

Callie opened her eyes. Misha stood in the doorway, frowning, his eyes raking over her in concern.

"I'm fine."

"You don't appear fine."

Callie sighed. "I appreciate everything you've done for me and the boys. But I'm not a charity case."

Misha's frown turned into a scowl. "I don't know what you're talking about."

"I've been taking care of my boys fine up to this point."

Misha moved closer. "I know you have. Your boys are wonderful, and that's all due to you."

"But now we're living in the demon compound, and your cousins helped us move, and Kyle brought dinner, and now Talia shows up with food that she doesn't want me to pay for—"

Misha held up his hands in front of her like he was trying to calm a wild animal. "It's been a long day. I'm sorry I asked everybody to come over here without checking with you first, but I wanted to make you feel welcome."

"I get that, Misha. But you have to understand that I need to remain in control of my life. As much as I appreciate everything you and the clan are doing, we don't know what the future will bring. A year from now, when the family who owns this house moves back from Russia, we'll be moving again. And I can't rely on you to help me every time we move. Next year at this time we could be living in another state."

Misha opened his mouth and then shut it again, as if rethinking what he was about to say. He cleared his throat. "You're in charge of your family, Callie. But you don't have to do this on your own. It doesn't mean you're weak, it means that you care enough about your boys to let others help you."

Callie pulled money out of her wallet and stood. "I can't teach them about their demon side, but everything else is my responsibility."

Misha nodded. "Agreed. I will try not to overstep my bounds, but I can't promise that I won't screw up again. Deal?"

Callie looked up into his ridiculously beautiful, ice-blue eyes. "Deal."

This was for the best. Callie needed to lay down ground rules now or she would lose control of the situation. The last time she lost control was with the boys' father. She wouldn't let anyone else take over her life again. For the sake of her boys and her own well-being.

CHAPTER 15

Callie took a deep breath as she set her laptop on the large table. The BSR team would arrive shortly, and with the number of people attending the meeting, they had moved from the temporary immigration offices to the community center meeting hall to accommodate everyone. She wiped her sweaty hands on her pants.

She was nervous for two reasons. One, she hadn't seen Misha or the rest of the BSR team since she had her move-in meltdown the other night. They had left rather quickly after she came out of her bedroom. Hopefully they hadn't decided she was an ungrateful bitch.

The second reason her nerves were on high alert was because Naya was supposed to attend the meeting. The same woman—female—that, according to Kyle, Misha had a crush on. Not someone she was looking forward to meeting.

Aleksei, Doyle, and Boris took seats at the table just as the BSR contingent of Misha, Jean Luc, Kyle, Talia, and Jason walked into the room. Greetings were exchanged, and Aleksei started the meeting.

"We're here to have a preliminary discussion about what we'll report to the Council. What has your team found out so far about the vandalism?"

Jean Luc leaned forward. "We have very little to go on. We interviewed the neighbors around the halfway house, and no one reported seeing the vandals. We have installed cameras at the house now, but there has been no activity."

"And the offices?" Aleksei asked.

Misha opened the folder in front of him and handed out papers. "The images from the security camera were wiped, except one blurry frame. I ran a number of programs to see if we could clean up the resolution. After a couple days, we've come up with this."

Callie looked at the picture in front of her. The man was large, with black hair and what looked to be a goatee. It was hard to make out any specific facial features.

"This is the best the software can do. Unfortunately, this image is not something I can run through the facial recognition program. The best we can hope for is that somebody will recognize him."

Kyle looked up from the picture. "He doesn't seem familiar to me. Does anybody else recognize him?"

Aleksei shook his head.

Boris set the picture down. "I will show it to Mother. She knows everyone. If anyone could recognize him, it would be Irina."

"What about you, Doyle?" Kyle asked. "You still have connections to the seedy underbelly of the supernatural world, don't you?"

Doyle's eyebrows shot up. "Seedy underbelly? You know I've been legit for a while now, Kyle. Ever since you offered me this job."

"I know. But that doesn't mean you don't still have connections on the street."

"I'll see what I can find out."

Kyle steepled her fingers. "Okay then, are we still on target for the next group to arrive?"

"Yes," Aleksei said. "The halfway house vandalism set us back slightly, but it shouldn't stop us from meeting our original timeline."

Callie typed steadily on the keyboard as she took notes. Her laptop beeped a low battery message and she cursed under her breath. She had forgotten to charge it earlier. Callie stood, and Aleksei stopped talking to look at her.

"I'm sorry. I have to go grab the power cable for my laptop I'll be right back."

Callie walked across the large space and stumbled to a stop. She gaped at the wall as it started to ripple like running water. She looked back over her shoulder, but no one seemed surprised that the wall seemed to be melting.

"It appears that Naya decided to join us," Aleksei drawled.

Callie faced the wall again as the rippling grew to the size of a door. Moments later, a woman walked through the wavy air. And what a woman she was. She wore a black jumper with armor built into the chest, arms, and legs. Her dark hair was plaited down her back, and she held a long staff in her hand.

This was Naya?

Gorgeous, fierce, tall, and purple! No wonder Misha had a crush on her. God, she couldn't begin to compete with a purple Angelina Jolie look-alike.

"Sorry I'm late. I had to deal with a disagreement."

"What sort of disagreement?" Aleksei asked.

"More demons are questioning the plan to come to earth."

"Why?" Kyle blurted.

"Much like the protesters you have here on earth, certain demons in the realm do not wish for things to change."

Boris frowned. "The Council will not like hearing this."

Aleksei tapped his fingers on the table. "The Council doesn't like to hear much of anything."

"Maybe so, son. But without their support, we'll be unable to bring others to earth."

Aleksei stood and headed over to Naya, who had walked up next to the table. "Can your guard control the protestors?"

"Yes, for now. We need to make absolutely sure the next group can come to earth. If we continue to show the realm that moving here is a reality, the protests should die down."

"And we need to be able to demonstrate to the Council that the realm demons aren't all out to destroy us." Aleksei gestured to the empty chair between them. "Take a seat and we can bring you up to speed on what's been happening."

"I'm fine standing."

"Must we always disagree?" Aleksei asked through what looked like clenched teeth.

Naya shook her head, but then flinched.

Aleksei's eyes tightened on her. "What's wrong? Wait—are you bleeding?"

Naya lifted her hand from her side, and green liquid ran down her palm.

Callie gasped. *Was that blood?*

Kyle jumped to her feet. "You're hurt!"

Everyone else jumped to their feet as well. Callie looked over at Aleksei, who gripped the back of the empty chair as if to stop himself from grabbing Naya. "You need to go to the infirmary and have the doctor examine you," Aleksei demanded over the commotion.

Naya shook her head again before grimacing slightly. "I'm fine. This can wait."

"You need to be looked at now," Misha argued.

Aleksei sighed, although he looked far from calm. "We know you can handle the pain, warrior woman.

But you're dripping blood everywhere. Go get sewn up in the infirmary."

Naya scowled at him. "Your concern for my well-being is overwhelming."

Aleksei's eyebrows shot up. "You don't strike me as someone who wants to be coddled."

"What is coddled?"

"It means babied."

Her eyes narrowed. "No."

"For once we agree on something. Kyle, will you please escort Naya to the infirmary?"

"I'm going, too," Misha announced.

Kyle and Naya left the room with Misha hovering close behind them. Everyone else sat back down...with the exception of Aleksei.

"Is she going to be okay?" Callie asked.

"She'll be fine," Aleksei answered, although his knuckles had turned white from the grip he had on the back of the chair.

After a moment Aleksei unclenched his fingers and paced next to the table. "Naya will stay here for a few days until she recuperates. We've suggested she spend more time here, and she has always rejected the idea, but she needs to learn more about earth and how to turn into her human side sooner rather than later."

Doyle interjected. "We should probably assign a mentor to her like we have with the other realm demons who've come to earth."

Callie looked at the notes on her laptop and saved them in case her battery died. She wouldn't be surprised if Misha volunteered for that role.

Aleksei stopped his pacing and came to a stop next to Callie's chair. "I think Callie can be her mentor for a couple of days."

Callie stopped typing. "Me? But I'm not a demon."

Aleksei shrugged. "She already knows how to be a demon. Naya needs someone who can teach her about earth. Plus you can explain to her how the immigration process works on our side so she can communicate it to those in the realm who'll listen to her."

Callie's stomach rolled and bounced like a tumbleweed while Aleksei kept talking. She had hoped to avoid Naya as much as possible. Petty? Yes, but sometimes you can't control your emotions.

"Callie, you didn't answer me. Do you have time to work with Naya?"

Now was her chance to make up an excuse...but she couldn't do it. The clan had done so much for her, she couldn't back out now.

"I'll make the time."

crap Crap CRAP

The words scrolled across her computer screen as if her fingers had minds of their own.

Misha paced outside the closed door of the examination room. He couldn't believe Naya had behaved as if nothing was wrong. She was bleeding, for Fate's sake.

"Mish, stop pacing," Kyle barked. "You're making me dizzy."

He mumbled a Russian curse word and kept on pacing.

"Eh, eh, eh... That was a creative one. You forget you taught me how to swear in Russian. Naya will be fine. She walked here, for goodness' sake, and the doctor said the cut on her side isn't deep. They'll stitch her up and then her demon metabolism will heal her in no time."

Misha spun to face Kyle. "She was attacked. She shouldn't go back to the realm."

"Good luck with trying to stop her."

Misha pinched the bridge of his nose. "I am so tired of dealing with stubborn females."

Kyle's mouth quirked up. "Why do I have a feeling we're not only talking about Naya right now?"

"Who else would I be talking about?"

"How about Callie?"

Misha could feel his blood pressure rise at the sound of her name. "All I'm trying to do is protect Callie and her sons. I don't think I've done anything wrong."

Kyle sighed. "Misha, Callie almost had a fit because Talia bought her some groceries. What do you think she's going to do when she finds out she's staying in your house?"

"Babushka said the same thing."

"Well, she's right."

Misha shrugged. "It's not like I'm homeless. Besides, I don't live there anyway. I still have my apartment."

"That's not the point. You lied to her. We have all lied to her."

"Because she is a stubborn woman like you and Naya. She would not have moved here if I told her the truth. Whether she knows it or not, she and the boys need the clan."

"All I'm saying is you better be prepared for her reaction when the truth comes out."

"If I've been able to deal with you for the last decade, I think I can handle Callie."

Kyle grimaced. "I'm not so sure about that."

Misha began pacing again. Was it so wrong to want to protect people? Wasn't that why he first joined the Bureau of Supernatural Relations?

The exam room door opened and the clan doctor walked into the hall.

Misha took a step toward him. "How is she doing?"

"Fine. Luckily she was wearing the armor, which blocked most of the knife strike, or her injuries would have been far worse. I sutured her side and told her she should take it easy, but I don't think she's going to listen to my advice."

"Can we see her?" Kyle asked.

"Yes. Maybe you can talk some sense into her."

Misha and Kyle found Naya sitting on the exam table. She had already put her armor back on.

"What are you doing?" Misha demanded.

Naya's right eyebrow rose. "Getting dressed."

"You won't need your armor here."

"But I will need it in the realm, where I'll be returning shortly."

Before Misha could argue there was a slight knock at the door.

Callie stood in the doorway. "Sorry to interrupt." She looked at Naya. "I'm glad you're okay."

"Is the meeting over already?" Kyle asked.

"They're wrapping things up now. Aleksei asked me to come talk to you guys about…well, Naya." She lifted her hand in a small wave. "I'm Callie, by the way. We didn't get a chance to meet earlier, what with you appearing through the shimmery wall and then bleeding and all."

"Hello, Callie," Naya said. "What has Aleksei proclaimed should be done with me?"

"Well, he thinks you should stay on earth for a couple days to recuperate. And while you're here, you can learn more about the immigration steps here, and you can learn how to turn into your human side."

Naya scowled. "For some reason Aleksei seems to be uncomfortable with me staying in my demon skin all the time."

Misha nodded. "For once I think my brother's right."

"And if I don't agree with you and your brother?" Naya asked.

Callie interrupted. "Yeah. About that. Aleksei says if you don't agree...and he wasn't holding his breath—his words, not mine—that I should tell you the portal is closed on the earth side until further notice. Whatever that means."

His brother had a lot of guts to go up against Naya, but in this instance Misha agreed with Aleksei's high-handedness.

Naya's eyes tightened. "And what am I supposed to do here in the meantime?"

Misha could teach her about earth. It was a perfect opportunity for him to spend time with her. He opened his mouth, but Callie spoke first.

"Aleksei asked me to be your mentor for the next couple of days. I can tell you about earth, and you can help me put together transition plans for the next group of realm demons."

Damn. On second thought, maybe he didn't like Aleksei's proclamations.

Naya blew out a hard breath. "Very well. I will contact my second-in-charge and let him know I will be staying for a few days."

Misha grinned. Naya was staying on earth. And he needed to suck it up and actually talk to the female. Hovering over her in the infirmary was not the foundation for a lasting relationship.

CHAPTER 16

Callie put two bowls of cereal on the table. "Matty, Luke, you need to come eat or you'll be late for day care."

The boys ran into the room and took their seats. Callie set two glasses of juice, orange for Matty and apple for Luke, on the table.

The toaster popped behind her, and she grabbed the piece of toast and slathered it with peanut butter before sitting down at the table next to her gigantic cup of coffee.

She would need every ounce of caffeine. She had tossed and turned all night because she was scheduled to spend the day teaching Naya about earth. She sat for several minutes nibbling on her toast. For starters, what should be the first subject they worked on?

"Momma?" Matty said.

"What, baby?"

"You're thinking really hard."

Callie put her coffee down. "I'm what?"

"Thinking. When you can't figure something out, you get those lines between your eyebrows."

Luke ran his fingers up and down his forehead as if to demonstrate.

Callie smiled at her too-observant sons. "I'm trying to work out a puzzle in my head."

"Can we help?" Luke asked.

"Yeah. We like puzzles," Matty piped in.

"I have to help teach somebody who doesn't understand our ways about...well...everything."

"One of the demons from the other world?" Luke asked.

Callie gaped at him. She hadn't told the twins about the realm yet. They had been doling out information in bits and pieces so as not to overwhelm the boys. "How did you know about that?"

The boys responded with identical twin shrugs before they looked at each other as if to decide who would speak. Luke must have won the mental coin toss.

"We've heard grownups talking about it. We may be little and not know all the words, but our ears still work."

Well. Didn't that just put her in her place. "Yes, I'm going to be training a demon. Someone who doesn't understand anything about our world."

Matty nodded. "Like a little kid."

"Yeahhhh!" Luke said. "Are you thinking what I'm thinking?"

"Yep," Matty said as they both got up and ran toward their room.

"Where are you two going?" Callie called.

The boys ignored her and kept going. Callie sighed as she stood and cleared the table. She couldn't imagine what they were getting into now.

Right before she hollered for them again, they came into the room, each carrying a stack of books. They plopped them on the table and grinned up at her.

Callie took a closer look, and couldn't help but smile. They were the picture books she used to teach the twins back before they started school—animals, food, letters, numbers, machinery, colors—a variety of basic things that would lay the foundation for what she needed to teach Naya.

"What a great idea!"

The boys' chests puffed up at her praise. They were definitely going to give her a run for her money when they got older.

An hour later, Callie sat waiting for Naya in a small conference room with a table and four chairs. Callie hoped meeting with her away from the bustle of the immigration offices would mean there would be fewer interruptions.

The door opened and Naya stalked in still wearing her realm soldier gear. Callie gestured to a chair across from her, and Naya took her seat. Being so close to the formidable female sent Callie's self-doubt into a tizzy. Naya's skin was deep purple, which Callie had seen yesterday. What she hadn't realized was that her eyes were entirely jet black, no white at all, and no other colors. And right now they were staring unblinkingly at Callie. She took a deep breath.

"Good morning, Naya. Did you sleep well last night?"

"It's hard to sleep well in new surroundings."

"I hope to explain about our surroundings so you become more comfortable in them. Before we get started, can I ask you a few things?"

"Yes."

"On your visits to earth, have you ever left this compound?"

"No. I've never left this building, actually, other than through the connected walkways. I've come for several Council meetings and discussions regarding the immigration plans."

Wow. This was even worse than she thought. "Can you tell me about your realm? Describe your life to me?"

"Why do you want to know about the realm?"

"Because if I know what your world is like, it will help me tell what you need to know about earth."

"Our world is not advanced like here. The realm does not allow us to use technology. We live much like earthers lived hundreds of years ago. We live in crude huts and cook over an open flame. We hunt and grow our food. The border patrol lives in what is called the in-between. Our job is to patrol the realm to maintain peace and stop the realm demons from coming to earth."

"How do you know what earth was like before?"

"Books. The previous leader of the patrol traveled back and forth to earth to report to the Demon Council, and he would bring back books for me. That is how I learned English and several other languages.

"According to Kyle, the books I have are what she calls classics. When I travel here now, she sends books back with me. They are very different from the ones I previously read."

She could just imagine what books Kyle had decided Naya needed to read.

"If you don't have technology, how do you move between worlds?"

"Portal jumping can be done in two ways. A small number of guards have been given the ability to jump between dimensions. This was provided by the demons of earth centuries ago."

"And you are a guard because your family volunteered?"

"My grandparents agreed to protect earth from the realm demons, as did my parents."

"What is the second way a portal can be formed?"

"Certain demons have the power to jump between dimensions. They're called Abstatholm. They are rare, but they exist in the realm, and are able to travel to earth."

"Wow."

"Can I ask you something now?" Naya asked.

"Sure."

"How did you end up working for Aleksei and demon immigration?"

"You mean, how did a human come to be working here?"

Naya nodded.

Callie took a breath before responding. "My twin sons are half demon."

"Your mate is Shamat?"

"I don't have a mate. The twins' father never told me he was demon, and he was killed before the twins were born. I didn't even know the boys were part demon until my son conjured a fireball."

"That must have been a shock."

Callie chuckled. "I'll say. Now I can laugh about it, but then I was terrified. I didn't know *what* was going on. Luckily, a shifter woman friend contacted the Bureau of Supernatural Relations, and that's how I met Kyle, Jean Luc, and Misha. Even though I don't know what clan the boys are from, the Shamat clan very generously adopted us as honorary members. I work for Aleksei, and we live in the compound so the boys can learn about their powers."

Callie reached for the books on the chair next to her and placed them on the table. "And speaking of my sons, it was their idea to let me borrow their books to help me teach you about our world. Maybe you won't need them if you've been reading."

Naya picked up a picture book about food and started to page through it. "No, this is perfect. Much of the time when I read, I don't have a point of reference for what the author has written about. I read a story recently that spoke of a giraffe. I couldn't figure out what it was."

Callie reached for the book with animal pictures. "We'll go over animals as well. Once we have gone through the books, we'll move on to Google."

"Is Google an elder?"

Callie smiled. "Not in the way you're thinking, but it can answer almost any question you ask it. It will really blow your mind."

Naya's eyes widened.

"Blow your mind is an expression. It means you might be overwhelmed by how much information you find."

"I've been overwhelmed since I went to Irina's house last night, and this morning when Irina asked me what I wanted to eat, I didn't know what anything was." She shuddered. "I won't be eating eggs again any time soon. It bled yellow when I poked it with the eating utensil."

"No sunny-side-up eggs for you. Let's try you on scrambled next time. Sorry, I bet you have no idea what I just said."

Naya looked down at the pictures of food again. "We should probably get started," the gorgeous female said. "Thank you for helping me.

Callie couldn't suppress her grin. It was hard not to like Naya. "No problem."

————————

"We have a problem," Kyle said.

Misha frowned at his petite team member's statement. "What type of problem?"

Kyle shook her head. "Let's wait until your grandmother gets here to have this conversation."

Misha jumped to his feet and started to pace the BSR's back office. "Babushka! Why is she coming here? Why has she left the compound? What—"

"Calm down, big guy. Irina is fine. What I should have said earlier is that *you* have a problem and it's time that we talked about it."

Misha looked over at Jean Luc, whose right eyebrow rose slightly.

"Are you in on this?"

"*Non*. But I will remain here to support you."

Kyle chuckled. "More like you need to be able to tell Talia what happened since she's not here."

Jean Luc's eyebrow rose a little bit more, but he didn't deny it. *Traitor*.

Before Misha could comment, the office door opened and Babushka came in, followed by her chauffeur, Grigori. In reality, Grigori was also Babushka's bodyguard when she left the compound. If his father had his way, his grandmother would never leave the safety of the compound ever again, but she would have none of that. Grigori was their compromise.

"Thank you, Grigori. Can you wait for me in the front office?"

Grigori's eyes lit up, and Babushka winked at him before he left the room.

What in the world? "What was that about?"

His grandmother chuckled. "Grigori has a bit of a crush on Dolly."

Kyle whistled. "Wow, he must like a challenge."

"How do you think he got this job? Boris interviewed a dozen family members before he found one who was actually willing to stand up to me."

Misha walked over to his grandmother and kissed her on the cheek. "What are you and Kyle up to, Babushka?"

Irina looked over at Kyle, who shrugged. "I didn't say anything, other than he is in trouble."

Irina took a seat at the conference table. "Very true."

"Why am I in trouble?"

Irina nodded for Kyle to continue.

"Mish. You are missing out on an opportunity. For the first time, Naya is staying here on earth—in your clan's compound, for God's sake. Are you planning to spend some time with her?"

Misha's nerves danced. "She arrived only last night. I didn't want to rush things."

Kyle dropped her head to the table with a soft thunk before picking it up and thunking it again. "You can't be subtle with Naya. She doesn't do subtle. If you're going to throw your hat in the ring, you better do it loudly, and soon."

"What do you mean by that?" Misha asked.

"I made breakfast for Naya this morning at the community center," Irina said. "While we were in the community kitchen, no fewer than five males dropped by for breakfast. All of them single, and all of them striking up a conversation with Naya."

"What!" Misha sputtered.

"You can't be surprised," Kyle said. "Naya is gorgeous. Hell, if I wasn't involved with Dalton and I swung that way, I would go after her myself."

"I agree with Kyle, Mikhail. If I was six hundred years younger and swung that way—"

"Babushka! There will be no swinging for you! None."

His grandmother chuckled. "Our point, my precious grandson, is that you are in lust with Naya. Part of love does include attraction, but it is more important that the personality attracts you. According to Kyle, other than last night when you escorted her to the clinic after her injury, you have not had a conversation with Naya. How are you supposed to determine if you are in love with someone if you have only looked at them from afar?"

Misha had nothing to say for himself. As usual, his grandmother was right, although having a conversation with his grandmother about his love life, or lack thereof, was disconcerting to say the least.

He looked to the only other male in the room for support. "What do you think, vampire?"

"I think you have not had an issue butting into everyone else's love life, so I feel I must tell you to speak to the female. You have never had trouble speaking to any other living being we have dealt with in the past. It is not time to lose your nerve now."

So much for male solidarity. "See if I have your back the next time Talia disagrees with you."

Jean Luc shrugged in his nonchalant way. "You normally support Talia's position in our arguments anyway."

Misha glared at him. "Because she's normally right."

"And I think I know what Talia would say right now if she were here." Jean Luc cleared his throat and placed his hands on his hips. "Listen up, you lunkhead demon. It's time to put on your big-demon pants and talk to the female, or you'll spend the rest of your life wondering what would have been."

Misha blinked at his teammate.

"Holy crap, Jean Luc," Kyle breathed. "That is exactly what Talia would have said. It's like you're channeling her."

"I know what she would say because I love her." He looked pointedly at Misha. "Is that not something you want as well, *mon ami*?"

More than he could ever express, especially watching how happy his teammates were now that they were in loving relationships.

"I'll talk to her," Misha said. "I'm working with the twins today. Afterward, I'll make a point of searching her out."

Babushka and Kyle high fived at his announcement, and Jean Luc actually smiled slightly, showing a bit of fang.

CHAPTER 17

Callie laughed as her boys tried to do cartwheels on the training center mat. They were beyond excited, because Misha was coming to train them today. And to be completely honest with herself, she was excited to see him as well.

The door opened, and Kyle entered the large room. She waved at the boys and walked over to Callie. "Misha will be here in a bit. Or at least I hope so. Boris waylaid him about something. How did your meeting with Naya go today?"

"Good. I think I might have overwhelmed her a bit, but she is so eager to learn about earth."

"She's trying on some clothes I brought her. I hope to get her out of her warrior woman costume while she's here."

"We talked about clothes today. I think she was shocked to learn we don't wear armor when we're outside."

Kyle frowned. "I'm not surprised. I've been to the realm, and it's not a fun place."

Callie gaped at her. "You've been to the realm?"

"Yeah, I was chasing a realm demon and ended up getting sucked through a portal. That's how I met Naya. She saved Dalton's and my asses."

"Dalton?"

"He's my..." Kyle pinkened slightly. "My significant other. He works for the FBI and sometimes helps us with cases. Right now he's in Chicago on a case. So, I was wondering if it would be okay with you if I introduce Naya to the boys?"

Callie hesitated for a moment. She had told the boys about Naya, and how much she appreciated their books, but talking about a realm demon and seeing one in purple technicolor were two different things.

"I totally understand if you're worried about the boys. They've had a lot thrown at them in the past few weeks."

"They have, but they have been so accepting of everything. Feel free to bring Naya back. I'll introduce her to Matty and Luke."

Kyle smiled. "Great. How about this? Meet us in the community kitchen after the training. I know Irina restocked the freezer with ice cream this week. The boys can have a treat, and we can introduce Naya to one of my favorite desserts."

"Sounds like a plan," Callie said before Kyle left.

The boys ran over to Callie.

"Isn't Kyle staying for our training?" Luke asked.

"Kyle is going to bring Naya here to meet you later. I told you about Naya at dinner tonight."

"The one you're teaching with our books?" Matty asked.

"Yes. You should probably know that she doesn't look exactly like us, but I don't want you to be scared. Her skin is purple, and her eyes are all black."

"Cool!" the boys said.

Why was she not surprised that they took it in stride? Why couldn't adults be as accepting as children? The world—both worlds—would be a much better place.

A few minutes later the door opened and Misha sauntered in.

"Hello, my young friends, are you ready to train?"

"Misha!" the boys hollered as they scrambled toward him.

Callie muffled a laugh as the boys grabbed onto Misha's legs. Misha laughed his belly laugh and ruffled their hair before taking them to the mats to begin training.

Misha watched Luke pick up the two ping pong balls with his mind and float them in the air. "Now try to move them back and forth."

The balls wobbled slightly before they started moving in a circle.

"That's great, Luke." And it was an amazing feat for a seven-year-old. Misha really needed to figure out where Mark Stewart came from. Maybe it was time to have Doc do the boys' blood work to see if it would help identify their clan.

But before he could talk to Doc, he needed to talk to Naya. He had promised Kyle, Babushka, and his turncoat vampire friend that he would try to get to know her. On the way over to the compound he practiced small talk and chose things to discuss with Naya. But the more he thought about it, the more he knew it wouldn't work. He couldn't very well talk about current events, or even something as mundane as the weather to a demon who had no frame of reference to earth at all.

"Mr. Misha, can I stop now?"

Misha looked down at Luke, who seemed to be straining to keep the balls in the air. "Yes, Luke. It's wonderful that you can keep more than one object in the air." Enough of concentrating on his own worries. He was here to train the boys.

He turned to Matty and pointed to an enclosed area at the side of the training space. The area resembled a thin hallway with a bullseye on the far wall. The walls themselves were made out of fireproof materials.

"Matty, about a year ago you created a fireball at one of your soccer practices. Do you remember how you did that?"

Matty's eyes widened. "I'm not sure, Mr. Misha."

"Did you think about the fireball and it appeared?"

Matty shrugged.

"Do you remember what happened right before you made the fireball?"

Matty shook his head.

Misha turned to Callie. "Do you remember?"

Callie nodded. "I'll never forget. Matty was running drills with a soccer ball, and Luke kept stealing the ball from him. Matty yelled at him to stop. When Luke didn't listen, Matty stomped his foot, held out his hand, and a ball of fire appeared."

"I remember now," Matty said. "I wanted him to give me the ball back, so I made a ball of my own."

"So you were mad," Misha said. "Maybe it's similar to when you blow things up. Let's try this. Think about the sparkles floating in the air and form them into a small ball."

Matty concentrated on the air in front of him. After a few seconds his eyes went glassy, and he held up his hand in front of him as tiny sparks rose from his palm.

"Keep it up Matty, you're doing great."

The sparks glowed brighter before fizzling out until nothing but smoke remained. Matty dropped his hand down and kicked at the floor.

Misha ran his hand over Matty's head. "Don't get discouraged. Creating fireballs is a high-level skill. Even some adults have trouble with it."

Matty crossed his arms. "I bet you don't have trouble with your powers."

Luke piped up. "What type of powers do you have, Mr. Misha?"

Misha hesitated. He should have expected this question to come up. But he didn't have an answer prepared. Did he want to tell them the truth and risk that others would find out? He had spent centuries downplaying his powers. But he didn't want the boys to think he was ashamed of his powers, either. Wasn't that the point of all this? To teach the boys that being a demon was okay?

But there were too many other things to consider right now. He had to tell them something.

He looked over at Callie. The longer he hesitated, the more her gaze narrowed at him.

"I am very strong." He walked over to a set of weights and picked up a large barbell with one hand. The boys gaped at him and then started jumping up and down.

"You're like Superman," Luke exclaimed.

"Can you fly?" Matty asked.

Misha chuckled. "No, I can't fly. No leaping tall buildings in a single bound." He set the weight down. "I don't want you boys trying to lift any of these weights without supervision. Do you understand?"

"Yes, sir," they chimed.

Misha slapped his hands together. "Good. Luke, go grab some different items out of the storage chest and place them on the mats. I want you to work on picking up different weights and moving them around. In the meantime, I'm going to work with Matty to see if we can get the fireball to work."

Fifteen minutes later Misha announced they were done for the day. Luke had been able to lift several items of various weights. Matty had almost been successful with the fireball. The sparks actually started to take the shape of a ball before petering out. Misha made a point of praising Matty, since he could tell the little boy was frustrated.

The boys now lay on the mats like limp noodles. Callie walked over and looked down at both of them. "It's time to clean up."

The boys moaned.

"Okay, I guess that means you're also too tired for ice cream."

The boys' heads popped up.

"Ice cream?" Luke, Matty, and Misha said simultaneously.

Callie laughed, and Misha was happy that he'd contributed to her delight.

"We're going to meet Kyle and Naya in the community kitchen for an ice cream treat. Let's get the room picked up."

So this was Kyle's way of ensuring he didn't chicken out about talking to Naya. The boys raced through the cleanup while Misha stood next to Callie watching them.

"You are very good with them."

Callie's eyes widened. "Well, considering that I just bribed them with ice cream, I'm not so sure."

Misha gazed at her, wanting her to hear what he had to say. "Don't downplay yourself."

"I could say the same thing to you."

"What do you mean?"

"Maybe I shouldn't say anything," Callie said.

"No, tell me what you mean."

"It seemed like earlier when the boys asked you about your powers you weren't…"

"…truthful," Misha finished the sentence. This woman was too insightful for her own good.

"I'm sorry if I'm overstepping, or if the boys asked something they shouldn't have."

Misha rested his hand on her shoulder and turned her toward him. "You aren't overstepping, and your sons asked a perfectly legitimate question. You're right. I didn't tell them the full truth."

Callie looked up at him quietly, as if to let him collect his thoughts.

"I actually have several different powers, but I don't let most people know. Not even my family."

"Why?" Callie blurted.

Misha looked over to see that the boys still had a few more items to pick up, which meant he had time to explain.

"As you know, my father is the leader of the Shamat clan. Succession normally goes to one of the leader's children. I am the oldest. Then Aleksei, and then my younger brother, Sergei."

"So you'll be the next leader of the clan?"

"Birth order has nothing to do with clan leadership. It has to do with strength of our powers."

Callie gaped at him. "You're hiding your powers so you don't have to lead."

"Aleksei was born to lead this clan. He is a natural leader, which is why he is running the immigration project. It will help him smooth his rough edges before he eventually has to take over the clan. I'm sorry I wasn't honest with your boys."

Callie rested her hand on his forearm. "I understand. But I think you need to ask yourself if keeping this secret is good for you or your family. I have done nothing but lie for years. My name is a lie. My background that I have told people over the years is a lie. And I lied to you and Jean Luc and Kyle for a year about my imaginary husband. A year that my sons could have spent learning about their powers and who they are."

Callie's words pricked at his conscience. He was lying to his family, and to her as well. But before he could respond, the boys ran up to announce they were done. Matty grabbed Callie's hand and Luke reached for Misha's before they headed for the ice cream.

A few minutes later, they walked into the community center kitchen. Kyle and Naya hadn't arrived yet. Misha grabbed a stack of bowls from the cupboard and spoons from a drawer.

"Let's see what kind of ice cream Babushka bought." He opened the standup freezer and pulled out gallons of vanilla ice cream, chocolate ice cream, and strawberry ice cream. Then he went over and opened the door to the walk-in pantry. "All right, boys, let's pick out some toppings."

The boys hustled over to him as he pulled out cans and jars of nuts, sprinkles, chocolate chips, and a jar of unopened maraschino cherries. They set everything on the table, and Misha grinned at the boys' excitement.

"We're missing the most important part." Misha opened the refrigerator and nodded to himself. Leave it to his babushka to think of everything. He pulled out the can of whipped cream and jar of chocolate sauce and placed them on the table as well.

"I think it's okay to serve the boys while waiting for Naya and Kyle," Misha said.

Callie looked down at their anxious faces and chuckled. "I can tell I'm going to be outvoted if I say no."

The boys each made a dish, and Callie watched the twins closely. Which let Misha sneak more toppings in their bowls.

"Misha! That is enough whipped cream."

Misha winked at the boys. "You heard your mother. I think she needs some help with her sundae."

Callie looked down at the scoop of vanilla she had in her bowl. "I'm fine. I just want a small scoop."

"No, no, this will not do! You have to at least have some toppings on that, Callie. It's just wrong to eat naked vanilla ice cream," he said with a shudder. "Do you trust me?"

She looked up at his eyes. "Yes."

"Then hand over the bowl." He scooped chocolate ice cream into the bowl as well, and sprinkled the ice cream with nuts, chocolate chips, and sprinkles. Then he put a drizzle of chocolate sauce on each scoop before finishing off with the whipped cream. "Now *that's* an ice cream sundae."

They had just started eating their sundaes when Kyle and Naya walked into the room. Naya was wearing a pair of jeans and a peasant blouse, although her hair was still in a braid down her back.

The boys stopped their chatter. Misha took a breath. It was time for him to attempt a conversation with Naya. Maybe he would ask her to go for a walk with him after the ice cream. Although she couldn't exactly go outside right now since she was still purple. Even in the demon compound, they refrained from showing their demon side outside.

Callie quickly did the introductions. "Naya, this is Matty and Luke. Boys, this is Naya."

The boys stared at her with big eyes before Matty whispered, "Pretty."

Naya's face broke into the first real smile Misha had seen from her, and it was breathtaking.

"Thank you." Naya took a step closer and her smile faltered for a moment as she looked at the boys. But just as quickly, she started smiling again, although it now seemed forced.

He glanced over and saw Callie's face, and all thoughts of speaking to Naya abandoned his brain. Callie was frowning. She definitely had noticed Naya's reaction, as had Kyle.

Kyle spoke up. "Mish, why don't you show the boys the media room? They can eat their ice cream and watch a cartoon."

Misha wanted to argue, but he didn't think the boys should remain to hear about whatever was going on. He nodded to Kyle and quickly shooed the boys out of the room with their bowls.

Someone would tell him afterward. If he couldn't get Callie to do it, he would corner Kyle and force it out of her later on.

CHAPTER 18

Callie's stomach twisted as she watched Misha leave with the boys. Why had Naya reacted that way when she got near Matty and Luke? She waited until the boys were out of earshot before turning to Naya and Kyle. "Tell me what's wrong, Naya."

Naya shook her head. "Nothing's wrong."

Callie's heart thudded in her chest. "You're lying. Why did you react that way when you met my sons? If something is wrong with the boys, you need to tell me."

Naya's eyes softened. "They are not ill."

"Then what?"

"I don't know if I'm the one to tell you this."

"Tell me what?" Callie practically hissed.

"I sense realm demon in your sons."

Callie's breathing sped up. "I don't understand. Can...can you tell what type of demon the boys are?"

"As with Kyle, I am unable to tell what type of realm demon the boys are."

Callie's eyes widened as she turned to Kyle. "You're part realm demon?"

Kyle nodded.

"I don't understand. How can this be possible?"

Kyle grabbed her hand. "Remember how I told you I was working a case and got pulled into the realm?

During our investigation, we learned that certain realm demons have been traveling back and forth to earth for years now. They were running a demon trafficking business, bringing realm demons to earth and selling them as indentured servants."

"So the twins' father was one of the people involved in the trafficking?"

"Possibly," Kyle said. "It is very rare for female demons to be born in the realm. So some of the demons who were traveling back and forth to earth were trying to impregnate human females."

"For what purpose?"

"We don't know for sure. Normally the realm is toxic to humans, but when I traveled there, I didn't get sick. Maybe the idea is to have children who can be brought back to the realm and survive. Or maybe it was to prove that the realm demons can come to earth and continue their species. Which could explain why the boys are so powerful at such a young age."

Naya nodded. "Realm demons are extremely powerful. They have to be, in order to survive. In the realm, demons must develop powers early to protect themselves."

Callie closed her eyes to stop the stupid tears from escaping. What did this mean for her boys? Demons on earth were already protesting the immigration. What would they do if they found out her sons' father was from the realm?

"Callie," Kyle said, "everything is going to be okay."

"You don't know that for sure."

"I know I'm living proof that a half-human and half-realm demon can live on earth and blend in."

"And I will tell you about the different demon clans in the realm. It will help you understand your sons' demon sides better," Naya said.

"Everyone has your back, Callie. You don't have to do this on your own," Kyle said.

Before Callie could respond, Misha walked into the kitchen with a stack of bowls.

"Where are the boys?" Callie asked.

"They're fine. They're in the room next door watching Bugs Bunny. I wanted to find out what was wrong."

"You know how Naya can sense that I'm part realm demon," Kyle said.

"Yes." Misha's eyes widened as if a lightbulb went off. "The boys' father was from the realm."

"Yes," Naya said. "I can't sense which demon clan exactly, but they definitely have realm blood running through their veins."

Misha reached for Callie's hand. "Everything will be okay."

"That's what Kyle said."

"And she's right. At least now we know why they have such high-level powers. Nothing has changed. You and the boys are still welcome here."

Callie nodded since she didn't want to disagree with him. But Misha couldn't guarantee that they could remain there if the trouble escalated. She had spent her childhood and adult life taking care of herself and now her sons. And she wouldn't stop now.

Callie couldn't rely on anyone to protect them. Even a kind-hearted male with the prettiest eyes she had ever seen.

———————

Callie held open the door to her house as Misha carried the twins inside. They had both conked out while watching cartoons, and Misha volunteered to carry them home. He carried them with ease, Matty resting on his right shoulder and Luke on his left.

She led him to the boys' bedroom, where he laid them on their beds. Callie pulled Luke's shoes off and helped the half-asleep boy change into his pj's. She was surprised when Misha did the same for Matty.

Once both boys were tucked in bed, Callie expected Misha to leave, but he walked into the living room instead.

"How are you doing after what you learned about the boys?" Misha asked.

"I don't know yet. It's a lot to take in."

He walked over to look at the pictures of the boys she had lining the mantle.

"You're really good with them," she said. "I'm surprised you're not married with children of your own."

Misha turned to face her, his expression sad. "I have been married before. My wives and I never conceived."

Wives? Dear Lord, did he have a harem or something? "You have more than one wife?" Callie blurted.

Misha's eyes twinkled. "Not at once. I was married three times."

Callie sat down on the couch. "Three? You look like you're in your mid-30s, and you've already been married three times?"

"I'm two hundred and sixty-five years old, Callie."

It was a good thing Callie was already sitting down. "You told me demons lived long lives, but I had no idea that you meant centuries. Will the boys live that long?"

Misha squatted down in front of her. "I'm sorry if I've upset you again. I would assume that the boys will live longer, but they're also half human, so that will weigh into it."

She nodded. "I'm okay. No parent expects to outlive their children, but I might miss a large part of their lives."

She gave her head a sharp shake to get rid of the maudlin thoughts. What mattered was that her boys would have long lives. "Tell me about your wives," she said.

Misha's eyes widened. She was a little surprised with herself for asking, but she had trouble understanding why he was alone.

Misha sat on the couch next to her. "My first marriage was when I was quite young. Back then it was quite normal for arranged marriages in the clans. My father arranged for Galina and me to be married. We cared for each other, but the spark was never there. I found out that before we married Galina was seeing another male, one her family didn't approve of. Samuel was a good male from a poor family, and it became clear that he and Galina were supposed to be together. We divorced, and Galina and Samuel ran away and got married. They celebrated their two hundredth wedding anniversary a few years back. The party their children threw for them was wonderful."

"Good for them," Callie said.

"Quite. Are you sure you want to hear about the rest of my pathetic love life?"

"Please."

Misha chuckled. "I like how you didn't argue about me using the word pathetic."

"I can't really make that judgment call until after I hear the rest of your story."

"Very true. Wife number two was what would now be called a rebound marriage. Natalia was a beautiful daredevil. I'm still half convinced she married me because everyone told us it was a mistake. It didn't take us long to realize our attraction had no substance behind it. We parted as friends."

"Can I ask where Natalia is now?"

Misha smiled. "The last I heard, Natalia was in Paris. But she could have moved on by now. She never stays in any one place very long."

His smile faded a bit and Callie held up her hand. "You don't have to tell me any more if you don't want to."

He shrugged. "You might as well here the rest of it, Callie. Have you heard the saying 'the third time is the charm'? I thought that was the case when I married Catrina. I loved her, and I thought she loved me, until she realized that I would not step up and claim the clan leadership when my father steps down. I tried to make it work…"

"What happened?" Callie asked.

"She made a pass at Aleksei."

"That power-hungry bitch!" Callie blurted.

Misha's mouth fell open.

Mortification in the form of a blush prickled along Callie's skin. She couldn't believe she had said that.

Misha's shock was quickly replaced by a chuckle. "Your reaction is very similar to Aleksei's when he told me what happened. So there you have it. Have I given you enough information to pass judgement?"

"You're not pathetic, Misha Sokolov. Far from it. Besides, with my track record, I shouldn't be passing judgement on anyone."

He frowned. "You are far from pathetic yourself, Callie Roberts. You are amazing. Those two boys in the other room are a testament to the woman you are."

A lump formed in Callie's throat at the fierceness in Misha's gaze. She had never had anyone rally around her. And even if friendship was all Misha could offer her, she would take it.

For now.

CHAPTER 19

Misha and Kyle walked into the back office of the BSR. Jean Luc, Talia, and Jason were sitting at the table as if waiting for them.

"How did it go?" Jean Luc asked.

"It didn't go at all," Kyle announced.

Misha wasn't sure what they were talking about. "How did what go?"

Talia sighed. "Your talk with Naya."

Naya? Oh, yes, he was supposed to talk to Naya after the training.

"They didn't talk at all," Kyle answered before he could.

"It wasn't exactly like I could ask Naya to go for a walk after we found out the boys are part realm demon," Misha protested.

"What!" Jason said.

Kyle plopped down next to him at the table. "We introduced Naya to the twins, and she sensed that they are realm demon like me."

"Callie was upset, so I walked her and the boys home after the training."

Kyle stared at him for a moment. "Right. Since the team's all here, why don't we plan out your next opportunity to spend time with Naya?"

Misha didn't believe in coincidence. "Is that why everyone is here, to discuss Naya and me?"

Misha glanced over at Kyle, who shrugged in faux innocence.

"Did you actually call them to the office?"

"No…I texted them. But they were already here."

Talia propped her chin on her hand. "I got a potential lead on the picture from the office break-in. One of my bounty contacts thinks he knows the male. He is supposed to call me tonight to give me the details."

"That's great. We need to figure out something before the Council meeting in a couple of days," Misha said. "Why didn't you call us?"

"Because we didn't know when we would hear from them, and we didn't want to interrupt your quality time with Naya," Jason responded before chuckling.

"Be careful, my friend," Misha warned. "We don't want to start comparing love lives. If that's the case, I'm going to call a certain beautiful doctor I know."

Jason scowled. "There's nothing going on between Sabrina and me."

"And that is a sad, sad state of affairs." Misha said.

Jean Luc stood. "Do not deflect, *mon ami*. We can only work on one emotionally stunted male at a time."

The room went quiet as everyone gaped at Jean Luc.

"What? I merely anticipated what Kyle and Talia would say next. I am attempting to move things along."

Kyle laughed. Talia stood and wrapped her arm around Jean Luc's shoulder. "So…you *can* teach an old vampire new tricks."

Kyle's laugh morphed into guffaws. After a few minutes, she wiped the tears from her eyes, and clapped several times, like a schoolteacher. "Enough frivolity. We need to help Misha prepare for his next meeting with Naya."

"I haven't scheduled the next meeting with Naya."

"*You* may not have." Kyle smiled. "But I did."

"And what is this meeting about?" Misha asked.

"I was talking to Naya earlier, and she really wants to learn how to change to her human form. That's not something that Callie is going to be able to teach her. So I volunteered you."

"Great thinking, Kyle," Talia said. "It'll give him the chance to talk shop, and then he can slip in some small talk on the side."

"Exactly. I'm glad someone appreciates the effort I'm making here."

A voice came from the doorway. "I see I can't leave you alone for a minute, McKinley, before you're getting into everyone's business."

Misha turned as Joe Dalton, Kyle's boyfriend, walked into the room with a wicked grin. He didn't bother acknowledging anyone else, just gazed at Kyle like she was the only person in the room.

Kyle popped up from her chair and was around the table so fast Misha would have sworn she traveled at vampire super speed.

Joe pulled her into his arms and kissed her, long and passionately. To the point that Misha started to hum and look away from the obviously private moment between Kyle and her mate.

After a moment, they came up for air and Kyle smacked Joe's arm. "Why didn't you tell me you were coming home tonight? I would have picked you up at the airport."

"It was a last minute thing. I wanted to surprise you."

She beamed at Joe—his teammate was actually beaming—and Misha couldn't keep a smile off of his own face. "It's good to see you, Joe."

Joe wrapped his arm around Kyle's shoulder and pulled her up against him while he exchanged greetings with the rest of the team. Then the team brought Joe up to speed on the case before Kyle and Talia told Joe all about Misha's nonexistent love life and how they were going to help him. Jason chuckled.

Misha bit back a moan. He wasn't even sure if he needed to be in the room anymore, since they clearly didn't require his input while they planned out his love life for him. All he needed was for his babushka to show up and his humiliation would be complete.

Misha trudged to the kitchenette to pour himself a coffee. Too bad he didn't have anything stronger to add. Before he could take a sip, Talia's phone rang.

"Yeah Nick, what have you got for me?" Talia listened for a minute. "Thanks. Yep, we know the neighborhood. I owe you one."

Talia hung up the phone. "Sorry for not putting him on speaker, but bounty hunters are a little paranoid. So the guy in the picture has been spending time on the west side, talking to some of the demons down there. He's been going by the name John."

Kyle sat up straighter. "Sylvia is still running the motel in that area, taking in stray realm demons. I bet she can give us some information about this guy or find someone who can."

"Well then, let's go pay her a visit," Misha said, thankful that they might finally have a break in the case, which meant they would stop talking about his nonexistent love life.

Sylvia agreed to meet them at a small Indian restaurant down the street from her motel. By the time she arrived, Misha had already polished off a basket of naan and an order of samosas, which were both quite tasty. He needed a late-night snack since he only had ice cream earlier.

Misha hadn't seen Sylvia in several months, but she still looked the same, and he smiled to himself about her unique style. She was a hippie throwback...long white hair in a braid, the flowing peasant dress, and clunky leather sandals...who was working to make the world a better place, one demon at a time. Her eyes widened when she saw the team waiting for her.

"This must be important if the whole team's here," she announced, without saying hi. Sylvia was always one to get down to business.

"Glad to see you and sexy cop are still going strong, Kyle."

Kyle laughed.

Joe gave Sylvia a quick kiss on the cheek. "You've always been on my side with this one."

Sylvia nodded. "You belong together. Even your energies read the same."

Sylvia looked at the rest of the team one at a time. If Misha had to guess, he would say she was trying to read their energy as well.

"Everyone else doing okay?"

Jean Luc nodded. "It is good to see you Sylvia. Unfortunately, this is not a social call."

"I'm assuming this has to do with some of the rumbling I'm hearing. I understand there's been some protests."

"As usual you're right," Kyle said. "We're trying to track down the demons responsible for trashing the halfway house and the immigration offices, and we got a tip we want to ask you about."

Misha pulled the picture out of his pocket and put it down in front Sylvia. "This image is of one of the people who broke into the office. We understand he may be spending time in this neighborhood."

Sylvia gave the picture a hard look. "Not a very good picture, but I have seen him."

"And have your sources told you anything about him?" Misha asked.

"Not much. I wonder if he is realm."

Kyle leaned forward. "Why would a realm demon want to stop the immigration? This is the best way to get the other demons to earth."

Sylvia ran her finger over the photo. "Maybe he doesn't want more realm demons to come to earth. I learned a long time ago that people are not predictable, and demons who come from a world the polar opposite of ours don't think the same way we do. What we might think is irrational makes total sense to them, and vice versa."

Talia spoke up. "Can you put some feelers out on the street to see what else you can find out about him? Without getting yourself in trouble, that is."

"I know how to stay out of trouble...sometimes." Sylvia chuckled. "Talia, glad to see you and Frenchie, here, are still together. Your energy is now linked together quite nicely." She looked at Misha. "You're like a big ol' cuddly teddy bear, Misha. There's something new bubbling around you. I'm seeing peaks of color. Do you want to share anything?"

"Nothing to share," Misha mumbled.

Sylvia's extended look told him she didn't believe a word of it, but she winked at him before homing in on Jason.

He held up his hands and shook his head. "I don't want to hear any of your energy psychobabble, Sylvia."

"I might be insulted, Jason, if I didn't know that you're just deflecting. All I was going to say is that your supernatural side seems to be stronger."

Jason's eyes widened, but he didn't say anything. Misha would have to make a point of spending some time with his friend to see how he was handling his shifter side. With everything that had been going on recently, he'd been neglecting Jason.

"How are the demons you helped adapting, Sylvia?" Kyle asked.

"Well, for the most part. When someone's motivated to find a better life, they're willing to challenge themselves. And from the stories I've heard about life in the realm, we have no comprehension of what a hard time really is."

Kyle nodded. "If it wasn't for you, we wouldn't have gotten to the bottom of the demon slave trade. Your model is the basis of our immigration plans."

Sylvia smiled. "I'm just glad you guys were willing to listen. Now we'll be able to help even more demons leave the realm."

"Which is why it's so important that we stop these protesters," Misha said.

"Let me guess." Sylvia frowned. "Your Council is getting nervous. Did they honestly think this process was going to happen without bumps along the road? I haven't met any bureaucrats, human or supernatural, that like to get their hands dirty. And the realm demons aren't the only ones who need to learn how to adapt."

Misha would make a point of speaking to both Aleksei and their father about Sylvia's words of wisdom. While they couldn't afford for the realm demons to expose the supernatural to humans, that didn't mean that the clans on earth shouldn't learn more about their realm counterparts.

CHAPTER 20

Callie beamed at her star pupil. Well, her only pupil, but Naya was a quick study. They had already reviewed Matty and Luke's books and now were talking about more complicated concepts like money.

"So you use these bits of metal and pieces of paper to buy things?"

"Yes. We used to barter like you do in the realm. Where someone would trade one thing for another. Now we use money."

"And how do you get this money?"

"Most people earn money from working. The job I do for immigration is paid. I'm then able to take that money and pay for food, clothes, housing, and other things."

Naya nodded, although Callie wasn't sure if she truly understood the concept. But it was a strange one to embrace when coming from a world with no monetary system. She didn't even want to think about explaining credit cards to her at this point in time.

Callie checked her watch. "I think that's enough for now. What are you doing after the lesson today?"

"Misha is meeting me here."

Callie's stomach dipped. It wasn't any of her business. She should just let it go. "Really? What for?" *So much for letting it go.*

"He's going to help teach me how to turn into my human side. I need to learn how to change if I ever want to leave this compound."

"Of course. It's fascinating to me that you each have two sides. I wonder if the twins are ever going to be able to take on their demon form."

"They might. You never know what their powers will become as they grow. You're more than welcome to stay to see how it works."

"Are you sure? I don't want to intrude."

"You're not intruding. You've already seen my demon side. My human side will probably be downright boring."

Callie highly doubted that.

The door opened, and Misha strode in. "Hello, ladies. Am I interrupting your training session?"

Callie shook her head. "We were just finishing up for the day."

"I told Callie you're going to help me with my human side, and I invited her to stay. She's curious about the process, in the event the twins can eventually change as well."

"Not a problem." Misha looked at Callie. "The boys might never change."

"I know. But it doesn't hurt to be prepared. I don't want to be totally caught off guard if it does happen."

Misha pulled out a chair directly across from Naya and sat down at the table. "For the clans on earth, demons are born in their human form and do not change until early adolescence, when they're about twelve or thirteen years old. It's almost treated like a rite of passage for some clans. My father taught me how to change for the first time. To change into your demon form, it's about understanding your human body and allowing it to expand into something greater. In your case, changing to human is going to be about pulling inward."

Naya frowned. "I don't understand."

"Here." Misha held out his hands across the table. "Let me try to help direct your energy."

Callie swallowed hard when Naya gripped Misha's hands. It was a petty reaction, she knew, so she tried to push away the seeds of jealousy, especially when Misha smiled at Naya.

"Sorry if I confused you. I think I was jumping too far ahead. Let's start with your breath. Close your eyes and inhale through your nose, holding the air in for the count of three before exhaling."

Naya closed her eyes and started her slow breathing.

Misha watched her closely. "Keep doing that, but as you inhale, imagine the air going to every part of your body, expanding your lungs, your heart, pushing itself down your spinal column and into your arms and legs, all the way to your fingers and toes.

"The breath you're pulling into yourself is energy, and it's expanding through your body, outwards to your skin. Now think about your skin. Let that energy spread across your skin. Now pull the energy inward. Absorb the energy on your skin into your body and hide it away."

Naya's skin started to change, turning from deep purple to lavender, but after a few seconds her skin returned to purple again. She opened her eyes and blew out a frustrated breath when she looked at her arms.

Misha squeezed her hands. "You're doing fine. I didn't expect you to be able to change immediately."

"What if you show me how you change to demon and back again? It might help me understand."

Misha's eyes widened at the suggestion. "I... Well..." Misha's words stuttered to a stop. Callie had never seen him at a loss for words before. He opened his mouth, glanced Callie's way, then closed his mouth again. She got the impression that his discomfort centered on her.

She pushed back the chair and prepared to stand.

"Where are you going?" Naya asked.

"I think Misha will be more comfortable if I leave."

Naya's gaze swung back to Misha. "Is that true?"

Misha let go of Naya's hands. "I'm not uncomfortable with you being here, Callie. But I don't want to upset or frighten you when I turn."

Callie sighed. "In the past year, I've learned that my twin sons are part demon. They conjure fireballs, move things with their minds, and can blow things up. A few days ago, we discovered that the twins aren't your normal earth demon. Instead their father originated from the demon realm. My current job revolves around helping realm demons relocate to earth, and I have been spending time with the amazing female across from you while she has been in her demon form. While I appreciate you being concerned, I don't think seeing your demon form is going to give me the vapors."

Misha's eyes twinkled. "Thank you for clarifying. I stand corrected." He looked down at his shirt. "When I turn into my demon form, I'm going to get bigger."

Callie stopped herself from gasping...which would have completely negated her whole I'm-not-a-weak-woman speech. But, dear God. He was going to get bigger?

"I'm not telling you because I think you're going to be scared, Callie. But I am explaining why I need to take my shirt off, since it's already tight. Otherwise I'll tear it during the change."

Callie didn't respond, especially when he reached up and pulled his shirt off over his head. There would be no words coming from her mouth any time soon. In order to speak, her brain would need to be functioning.

And it so wasn't right now.

Even when Misha was fully dressed, Callie could tell he was muscular. But seeing him in the flesh? He was amazing. He had a light dusting of blond hair on his chest—a chest that went on for miles—and now she had lost her words again...

He reached for Naya's hands and gripped them. Callie leaned forward. Maybe if she was closer, she would be able to feel his energy. He looked at her for a moment and winked before turning his attention to Naya.

Callie held her breath as the whites of his eyes disappeared as his eyes turned black. A moment later his hair darkened as his skin turned orange, starting on his head and rippling down over his neck chest and arms. Red markings appeared over the orange. And he hadn't exaggerated earlier. He had grown. Callie wasn't scared of him at all. Far from it.

He was glorious.

"Can you feel my energy, Naya?"

She nodded. "Yes. It surged through you a moment ago."

"Exactly. Now, as I change back to human. Pay attention to my energy, and see if you can mimic it."

Misha shrank slightly as his skin and hair changed back to their human colors. As he completed his transformation, Naya began to change as well. Her black hair lightened to a dark brown color, and her purple skin changed to a rich brown. Her eyes were also brown with specks of gold.

She was anything *but* boring. And from the smile on Misha's face, he thought the same.

"Very good, Naya. How did it feel?"

"Good. Thank you."

"Would you like to try a couple more times until you get the hang of it?"

"I think it would make sense."

Callie stood. "Thank you for letting me stay, but now it's time to get back to work. I have a long list to complete before the next immigration."

Callie didn't wait to hear if either of them responded. But she couldn't help but notice that they were still holding hands when she left the room. They looked good together, and after hearing about Misha's past, she decided maybe Naya was the right one for him. Would Misha really want to have a relationship with Callie? A human who would die centuries before he did?

An hour later Callie sat at her desk finishing up her work for the day when Aleksei came out of his office.

"Are you about ready to close up for the day?"

"Yes. I need to make a quick dinner for the boys before their training session with Misha."

"How is their training going?"

"Pretty good, actually. Matty is still struggling with creating a stable fireball."

"I remember how hard it was as well, and I was several years older than Matty. How are your training sessions going with Naya?"

"Good. As a matter of fact, Misha taught her how to turn into her human form today."

Aleksei's eyebrow rose. "Really? I didn't realize Misha was spending any time with her. He can barely say two words when he's around her."

"He didn't have any trouble today."

Aleksei frowned.

"Is something wrong? You are the one who's been pushing Naya to learn how to change."

Aleksei straightened his jacket sleeves. "Nothing's wrong. I'm glad that things are progressing."

The office door opened and Naya walked into the office in her human form. Aleksei gawked at her, his mouth slightly open, before he seemed to catch himself and closed his mouth into a thin line.

Naya scowled. "What have I done now?"

"Nothing. I'm glad to see you have embraced your human side."

"Misha is a good teacher. He invited me to watch him train with the boys tonight." She turned to Callie. "I want to make sure you're okay with that."

It appeared Misha had gotten over his shyness when it came to Naya. Callie batted away her jealous thoughts. "Of course. You're more than welcome."

Aleksei cleared his throat. "We were just talking about the training. Since Matty is still having trouble with his fireballs, I think I might stop in as well to see if I can help."

"How nice of you to offer, Aleksei. But I don't want to interrupt any plans you have for tonight."

"No problem."

Callie told Aleksei the time for the training and he left the office.

Naya waited while Callie shut down her computer and closed up for the day. They walked together out of the building and toward the day care facility. Naya looked around her with wide eyes and came to a stop.

"Are you okay?"

"Everything is so different here. Other than going through the walkway to Irina's house, This is the first time I've actually been outside the community center."

Callie gasped. "How silly of me not to remember. I'll tell you about things as we go. Why don't you come to my house for dinner? The twins would love to show you their playset, and they can answer more questions about what you're seeing outside."

Naya agreed, and they started walking again, Callie explaining different things to Naya along the way.

"How did the rest of the training go with Misha?" Callie asked.

"Good. I believe I can control the changes now, but Misha said I shouldn't leave the compound until I'm able to hold my human form for more than twenty-four hours."

"That makes sense. I'm glad Misha was able to help you."

"He is a good male."

Callie nodded since she was having trouble swallowing, let alone speaking.

Naya titled her head and stared at her like a lab experiment for a moment. "You like him."

Callie gawked at her. "What? No..."

Naya held up her hands. "I'm sorry if I have made you uncomfortable. I have a tendency to be too blunt. Living in the realm does not allow you to speak anything but the truth."

"I...do like him, but he doesn't see me in that way—" *Since he likes you,* she wanted to say, but she couldn't. It wasn't her truth to tell.

Naya's eyebrows rose. "What way does he see you?"

"As a charity case."

"I don't understand this term."

"Sorry. It means he is helping me because I'm a single mom who lost her job, and he thinks I need help with my demon twins." She blinked back tears. What happened to her earlier speech to Misha about being a strong woman with no vapors? Apparently tears were a different story.

Naya frowned. "I've seen you take care of your sons. You love them, and that's what matters. Demon boys are a handful, even for those of us who are demon. I would think any child would need to be raised with the help of a clan."

"I'm human. I can't do what you all do, and I'll die long before Misha does."

Naya eyebrows drew together in concentration. "Here on earth, is your longevity guaranteed?"

"I don't understand."

"Do all humans live to be elders?"

"No. Illnesses and accidents can take people earlier."

"So even when humans fall in love and mate, there are no guarantees they will be together until they both die."

"True."

"It's the same for demons. In the realm, long life is far from guaranteed. And here on earth, the same can be said. According to Aleksei, his mother has passed. Which means Boris is alone now. Do you think he regrets the life he had with his mate and the three boys they created?"

"Of course not."

Another head tilt from Naya. "Maybe the issue isn't the way Misha sees you. Maybe it's how you see yourself."

"What do you mean?"

"I mean, if you don't feel worthy to be in a relationship, then how do you expect others to see you that way?"

Callie opened her mouth and then closed it.

"I'm sorry—"

Callie cut off Naya's apology. "No. You're right. Blunt, but right." She stopped outside the day care center. "You're pretty observant for someone who's only been living on earth for a few days. I thought I was supposed to be teaching you."

Naya smiled at her. "We'll learn from each other."

"Sounds like a plan."

Callie pulled open the door to get her sons. She would think about what Naya said later...after she put the boys to bed tonight and she settled in her own bed. Alone.

CHAPTER 21

Callie watched her boys with pride. They were adorable. Matty and Luke each held one of Naya's hands as they walked to the training center. They pointed out everything around them like mini tour guides.

"Boys, we need to move a little faster or we're going to be late for your training."

"But Momma," Matty said. "There's so much that Naya needs to learn."

"I agree, honey. But she can't learn everything in one night. We'll see about having her over for dinner again soon, and you can explain some more things to her."

Luke chimed in. "We'll make sure to have more macaroni and cheese, but no hot dogs."

Callie smiled. Naya had not liked the hot dogs at all. Callie got the impression that she didn't eat much meat in the realm.

The boys pulled Naya along into the training area, where both Misha and Aleksei were waiting for them.

Callie stared at Aleksei for a moment. She'd never seen him out of the suit, but tonight he was wearing jeans and a pullover top. Misha was also wearing jeans, with a short sleeve shirt that accentuated his muscles. And now that she knew what his chest looked like it was hard not to focus on it. But she wasn't here to ogle either of the brothers.

The twins ran over to the men, and Naya stood next to Callie at the side of the room.

Naya looked around.

"The metal things are exercise equipment that you use to make you stronger and in better health. Here in the compound it's also used to train the children how to use their powers. I'm sure you don't have anything like this in the realm."

"We don't need anything like this. Surviving in the realm makes you stronger."

"When do you think you'll be going back?"

"After the Council meeting tomorrow night. It's time."

"I'm going to miss having you around," Callie said.

"I'll be back soon. I have much to learn about earth. The more I know, the better I can explain it to the realm demons. Maybe that will help stop the dissenters in the realm."

They watched Aleksei and Misha working with the boys. After about five minutes they stopped and Matty and Luke ran toward the door.

"Where are they going?" Callie called out to Misha across the room.

"Bathroom break," Misha replied.

Callie sighed. "I told them to go the bathroom before we came here."

"You are raising wonderful boys, Callie." Naya said. "You should be proud of yourself."

Callie turned to face Naya. "You're not trying to reinforce what you said earlier, are you?"

"A little bit. But that doesn't make what I'm saying any less true."

Before Callie could respond, the mirror behind Naya started to move right before a surge of light blinded her for a moment. A portal appeared.

Callie screamed.

Naya whipped around to face the portal and dropped into a fighter's stance. "Run!" She called over her shoulder as she changed into her demon form and grabbed a barbell pole in lieu of her staff. Three demons rushed through the portal into the room, each bigger than the last.

Callie froze. She told her legs to move, and when that didn't work, she started to beg them. Nothing.

The blue demon in the front attacked, and Naya swung her pole in an arc, slamming it into his arms.

Callie stumbled back, her legs finally working, but her movement caught the attention of a huge orange demon with a scar down his face. He ran toward her. Before she could scream again, she flew back as if a giant rubber band was around her waist, pulling her.

She landed in Misha's arms.

A fireball soared through the air and slammed into the chest of a gray demon with a machete-looking thing in his hands. Aleksei launched another fireball from his hand before slamming into the orange demon.

Misha set her down. "Go, Callie. Stop the boys from coming back into the room, and get help."

The boys! Oh, my God. Callie looked toward the back door they had left through.

"What about you?"

"I need to help Naya and Aleksei. Go!"

Callie ran out the door and down the hall to the bathrooms. She let out a sob of relief when she found the boys playing at the water fountain.

She grabbed their hands and pulled them toward the outside door.

"What's wrong, Momma?" Luke asked.

"We need to get help. Now."

Once Callie was safely through the doors, Misha ran toward the battle. Naya held her own against the demon she fought against, but Aleksei was holding off two at once. Misha picked up a barbell with his mind and flung it at the demon with the machete, hitting him in the shoulder.

The demon staggered back a few steps, and Misha helped another weight sail through the air. This time it hit the demon in the arm, and he howled, dropping his weapon. Misha picked up several hand weights with his telekinesis and launched a strategic strike. The demon raised his hands in the air to protect himself and backed through the portal.

The blue demon Naya fought couldn't deflect the blows she landed with the barbell pole she used as a temporary staff. He ran backwards through the portal as she swung the pole again.

At the same moment, Aleksei flipped the orange demon onto the ground, pinning him with his forearm against his neck.

"Why are you attacking us?" Aleksei demanded. "We're trying to help you come to earth."

"Lies," the demon choked out.

Shouts sounded behind them as Boris and several other clan members ran into the room. The shouts distracted Aleksei for a moment, and the demon punched him in the head, shoving him off and diving through the portal.

Instead of closing, flashes of light burst through.

"Get ready. More are coming!" Naya yelled.

"Everyone back away from the portal," Misha shouted.

Misha picked up a blue mat from the floor with his mind, set it on its side, and pushed it up against the portal opening. He gritted his teeth as he used his telekinesis to move a large piece of exercise equipment in front of the mat. Two other clan members pushed another piece of equipment against the mat as well.

The mat started bouncing as if someone was pushing it from the other side, and light burst around the outer edges.

"I can't hold it by myself!" Misha hollered.

Everyone ran over and pushed against the machinery and mats to help Misha.

"There's no one left here from their side. How can the portal remain open?" Aleksei asked as he strained against the machinery, helping to hold it in place.

Naya grabbed the machete lying on the floor, lifted her shirt, and placed it next to her rib cage.

"What the hell are you doing?" Aleksei yelled.

"I need to destroy my portal device. It's the only thing they could be using to lock onto this place."

"You're going to kill yourself." Aleksei ran over to her and took the machete from her. "Tell me what to do."

"The device is located under my third rib. Cut between the third and fourth rib."

Aleksei hesitated for a moment.

"Do it. I'll be fine."

"Hurry!" Misha yelled. The mat and the machinery pushed back into the room slightly. Even with the help of the others, he couldn't hold them back much longer.

Aleksei cut along her ribs, and Naya didn't flinch. When Aleksei reached for her side again, Naya shook her head. "If you try to extract it, I'll die. I have to be the one to touch it."

She cringed as she pulled a small silver cylinder out of her side.

Naya placed the device on the floor and picked up a hand weight, slamming it down onto the cylinder. Moments later the light bursts stopped, and the mat went still.

Misha bent forward, hands on his knees, sucking in large gulps of air. Thank the Fates the portal had closed when it did. He had almost tapped out his powers.

His father went into command mode, ordering sentries to be posted throughout the compound.

A voice called from the doorway. "It looks like you didn't need me after all," Irina said.

Boris glowered. "Mother. You were supposed to be in the bunker. What are you doing here?"

"I might be a thousand and twelve years old, but I'm still one of the most powerful telekinetics in the clan." She looked pointedly at Misha. "Or at least I used to be."

"Are Callie and the boys okay?" Misha asked.

Boris nodded. "Yes. She and the boys are in the bunkers with the rest of the children."

Misha's heart rate slowed down considerably at the news. He looked over to see Aleksei trying to help Naya with her bleeding side. She pushed his hand away. Although now that Misha got a closer look at Aleksei, he could see a large gash along the side of his face.

"Naya to the infirmary. Now," Boris commanded.

Aleksei smiled until their father turned to him next.

"Aleksei, you as well."

"I'm fine, Father. We need to regroup and discuss next steps."

"I agree. We can have that conversation in the infirmary while you are both being attended to."

"Yes, Aleksei. We know you're a warrior, but you're dripping blood all over the floor," Naya said with a straight face.

"Mother, will you please go back to the bunker and let Callie and the rest of the adults and children know everything is fine? I think it would be a good idea for them to stay there for a couple of hours until we make sure we'll have no more breaches."

"Of course, but I want to know everything that's discussed in your meeting."

"Yes, Mother." Boris then turned to Misha. "Call Kyle and Jean Luc and let them know what happened while we head toward the infirmary. I'm sure they'll want to join us. We have a lot to talk about."

Misha was pretty sure his father was referring to more than the attack, but now was not the time to discuss the secrets he had been keeping from his family.

CHAPTER 22

Callie looked at the large metal door for the hundredth time. She had to force herself not to get up and pace, but she didn't want to worry the twins or the other children who were locked in the bunker with them. Who built bunkers in this day and age anyway?

When she ran out of the training center earlier and told the first person she saw what was going on, he pulled out his phone and called the compound security. The next thing Callie knew, she and the twins were being led down a set of stairs to a large concrete room. Other children were also brought into the space. Teachers and day care workers put the children into groups and started to play games with them.

The twins sat next to her, still clutching her hands.

"Will Misha be okay, Momma?" Luke asked.

"And Naya and Mr. Aleksei?" Matty asked.

"I'm sure they're fine," she said, although she prayed she wasn't giving them false hope.

"Are the bad demons going to get us?" Luke asked.

She squeezed their hands. "No. We're safe here. There are guards outside the door, and I'm sure everything will be fine."

The door squeaked open, and Callie jumped to her feet pushing the twins behind her.

Irina stepped inside followed by her personal guard, Grigori, who carried two grocery bags. She held up her hands when everyone started talking at once.

"Everything is okay. The three demons who tried to get into the compound were not successful. Boris has asked that we stay here for a little while longer." She gestured to the grocery bags behind her. "I raided the community kitchen and brought the makings for s'mores. We'll have to melt the marshmallows in the microwave, but they'll still be yummy."

The teachers took the grocery bags into the little kitchenette with the children trailing behind.

Callie sucked in some big breaths to stop her heart from beating out of her chest as Irina approached her. "Is he...everyone okay?"

Irina smiled at her and then the boys, who were still clinging to her. "Misha is fine. Naya and Aleksei are fine as well. Boys, why don't you go see about having a s'more? I need to talk to your momma for a moment."

The boys looked up at her, and Callie nodded. "Everything's fine. Go get a treat."

The boys walked toward the other children. Callie waited until they were out of earshot before turning back to Irina.

"What do you want to say that you can't in front of the boys?"

"I didn't want to worry them. Naya and Aleksei are a little banged up from the fight, so Boris insisted that they get checked out at the infirmary. I know they're both fine because they argued about going. The BSR team should be here shortly, and they're going to have a discussion in the infirmary about next steps. I wouldn't be surprised if we hear from the Council leaders in the next couple of hours."

"That soon?"

"We may try and hide things from humans, but supernaturals don't hide things from each other very well. I'm sure by now news of the attack has started to get out to the other clans."

"What do you think will happen? Will they stop the immigration?"

"Not if our clan has anything to say about it." Irina gestured to the chairs, and Callie sat down with her.

"You have an amazing clan, Irina."

Irina beamed. "I know. And an amazing family. My son and grandsons are males with honor and heart. I thank the Fates every day for making them a part of my life. I didn't think they could surprise me anymore, especially Misha. But that just goes to show that I don't know everything. Not after seeing what he can do."

Callie reached for Irina's hands. "Please don't be mad at Misha for hiding his powers."

Irina's gaze sharpened on her. "You knew he had telekinetic powers?"

"I knew he had powers he wasn't telling anybody about."

"And yet he told you about them?"

She shrugged. "It just kind of happened. The boys asked him about his powers and I knew he hadn't told them the whole truth. So I called him on it."

Irina laughed out loud. "I really like you, Callie. Do you know why he's been hiding the truth?"

"I do. But it's not my story to tell."

"Fair enough. I'm just happy to find out that one of my grandsons inherited my powers."

Callie gaped at her. "You're telekinetic?"

"Yes. And a very powerful one. I actually saved my husband more than once back in the day when there was more fighting than negotiating between the clans." Irina patted her hand. "Speaking of negotiating, they should be sounding the all clear shortly. I think you should go to the infirmary to be a part of the discussion and put in your two cents. I'll watch the boys for you."

As much as Callie didn't want to let the boys out of her sight, she did need to be a part of the conversation. A conversation that could directly impact her sons' futures.

———————

Misha stood in the infirmary staring down the empty corridor. Aleksei and Naya had been shown into exam rooms, and Boris was making sure the compound was secure. Misha had already called and brought Kyle and Jean Luc up to speed. They would be arriving soon.

Right now he had this need — a compulsion really — to go to the bunker and check on Callie...and the boys, of course.

Steps came toward him, and he tucked his thoughts away as Boris walked around the corner and stopped in front of him.

"Everything is secure," Boris said.

"Naya and Aleksei are being taken care of as well."

Boris nodded. "We only have a few minutes before we need to discuss next steps, but before everyone else gets here, I want to tell you how sorry I am."

"About what?"

"For some reason you felt like you couldn't tell me the truth about your powers, which means I failed you somehow."

Misha's stomach dropped. "You've done nothing wrong. I...took the coward's way out instead of telling everyone the truth. You and I both know who the next leader of the clan is." He looked through the window in the exam room door and watched a nurse cleaning

Aleksei's wound. Aleksei had insisted the doctor take care of Naya first.

Boris followed his gaze. "You and I are going to talk about this in detail at a later date, when we are not dealing with attacking realm demons. But I don't think the discussion with your brother can wait. Do you?"

Misha shook his head.

"Go talk to him. You two need to discuss this alone."

Misha opened the door to the small exam room and walked inside. Aleksei didn't acknowledge him. After a few more minutes of awkward silence, the nurse finished up and said she would go find out when the doctor would be joining them.

After she walked out of the room, Aleksei looked up at him for the first time.

"Do you have something to say, brother?"

Misha opened his mouth and then hesitated. How could he explain?

When Misha didn't speak, Aleksei continued. "Why have you been hiding your powers?"

"Aleksei—"

"Were you going to spring it on us all one day. Announce 'The joke's on you, Aleksei, it's my clan now?'"

"That's not it—"

Aleksei held up his hand and stood. "Is it a pity thing, then? Poor Aleksei has always wanted to lead, so I'll hide the truth even if he isn't the rightful leader."

"No!" Misha roared, before taking a breath and lowering his voice. "Of course not. May I speak now?"

Aleksei crossed his arms before nodding.

"Back when grandfather and even father took over the clan, it made sense that they needed to have strong powers to lead. Now? Now, I think powers are less important than the ability and the desire to lead. I am not a natural leader. I have known this since I was a child. Yet if I felt there wasn't anyone to take over the clan once father is gone, I would step up and lead anyway. But I have also known since you were a child that you *are* a natural-born leader. I didn't want to take the opportunity to lead this clan away from you. I want the clan to have the best person to lead them, and I truly believe you are the best person."

Aleksei stared at him as if he was trying to read his thoughts to determine Misha's sincerity. After a few more intense moments, Aleksei spoke. "I appreciate your confidence in me. But you shouldn't have hidden the truth from your family. Your powers are part of you, and regardless of your feelings, clan law states that the progeny with the strongest powers is the leader."

"Then it is time to change the law," Misha said.

Aleksei's eyes flared. "I think you underestimate your ability to lead, brother."

Before Misha could respond, the door opened, and Kyle and Sabrina walked in.

"I can't leave you guys alone for a minute without you getting in trouble," Kyle said. "I called Sabrina in case the doctor needed backup."

"The clan doctor is with Naya now," Aleksei said.

"I'm surprised Joe isn't with you, little one. You two seemed connected at the hip since he came home last night."

Kyle blushed slightly. "He's out in the hall."

Sabrina walked over and took a close look at Aleksei's face. "That's a nice gash. Let me sew it up for you."

Kyle stopped next to Misha. "Make sure he doesn't end up with a scar, Sabrina. He thinks he's sexy now. If he has a scar on top of it, we won't be able to deal with him."

Aleksei grinned. "You think I'm sexy?"

Kyle sighed. "No. I said *you* think you're sexy."

Aleksei opened his mouth again, and Sabrina held up her hand. "Enough, you two. Aleksei, you're going to have to hold still while I do this, which means no talking. And I know that's not going to happen unless I kick Kyle out."

Kyle chuckled. "I was gonna go check on Naya anyway. The rest of the team is out in the hall talking to Boris. When you've finished stitching him up, we're going to discuss next moves." The smile left her face. "Boris has already gotten several calls from clan leaders. They're demanding an emergency videoconference in two hours. They don't want to wait until the actual meeting tomorrow to discuss what's going on."

"It didn't take long for the news to get out," Misha said.

Kyle opened the door. "I think the compound being attacked the day before the meeting to discuss the future of the immigration plan is too big a coincidence."

"Agreed," Misha said. "Someone's deliberately sabotaging this project, and it's time to figure out who they are, and how to stop them."

CHAPTER 23

Callie looked around at the tense faces in the conference room. The BSR team was there, along with Aleksei, Boris, Doyle, and Naya. Misha had set up a laptop at the end of the table and made sure its camera was working. She was so relieved to see he was uninjured.

Once Misha sat down, Boris started the impromptu meeting. "I think it makes sense for me to lead the conversation once we have the other clan leaders online. Kyle should sit next to me as well."

Aleksei frowned, but before he could argue, Kyle jumped in. "I agree. Sorry, Aleksei, but I don't think we want them to see your battered face when we're trying to defuse the building hysteria. By tomorrow, when they're here for the Council meeting, your demon metabolism will speed up the healing and you'll look much better."

"Very well. Let's quickly go over what you two should say."

Kyle and Boris looked at each other with raised eyebrows before turning back to Aleksei.

Callie tried to pay attention, but hysterics were setting in for her as well. Fear was a powerful motivator, and it often made people do stupid things. Forty-five minutes later she knew for sure that her theory applied to supernaturals as well.

She looked at the large screen on the wall where the Council leaders' faces appeared in squares with their name and clan name listed below. Talking heads that were too busy spewing their own opinions to really listen to what others were saying.

The Council leader in the upper right-hand corner, also known as Peter Solomon "Valtram," turned beet red as the meeting progressed. "I can't believe we are still considering allowing these realm demons to come to earth. They attacked your compound, yet you sit there defending them."

Boris shook his head. "I don't defend the ones who attacked us. I defend all the other demons in the realm who want nothing more than to come to earth for a better life. We cannot condemn thousands for what a random group of demons did."

"We don't know if it was random."

The arguing continued for another thirty minutes, until Mr. Upper Right-Hand Corner started demanding that they take the vote now to stop demon immigration.

The demon leader in the second row from the bottom by the name of Amelia Watkins "Dalmot" spoke up. "We need more facts before we can make a decision."

"Exactly," Kyle said. "We need more time to find out what's going on."

"Twenty-four hours should be plenty of time," Josiah Akers "Pavel" said.

While a few Council leaders, including Boris, rejected the twenty-four-hour time frame, the majority agreed to vote on the issue at tomorrow's meeting.

Boris disconnected from the videoconference, and the faces disappeared from the screen on the wall.

Callie looked down at the laptop in front of her. She had stopped typing meeting notes a long time ago. What was the point? All this work and promises to bring the demons to earth, and now they were going to take it away from them. And what did that mean for her boys?

Everyone at the table started talking at once until Aleksei shouted to be quiet. "We don't have much time. We need to split up and figure out who is behind this. I agree with Kyle that it is too coincidental that we were attacked the day before we were supposed to meet with the Council."

Misha leaned forward. "I agree as well. Naya, you didn't tell anybody about when we were meeting with the Council, did you?"

"No."

"Which means someone from earth had to tell them," Misha said.

"And it was as if someone locked onto Naya's portal device to keep the rift open," Aleksei said.

"Has anyone seen something like that before?" Kyle asked.

Naya nodded. "Guards are able to lock onto each other's coordinates. It's a safety mechanism to help in times of trouble."

"Do you think one of the guards is a part of this?" Jean Luc asked.

"I trust the guards with my life. It would more likely be that the rebels have gotten hold of one of the devices."

Aleksei's hands clenched into fists on the top of the table. "You mean they killed a guard to get the device."

"Possibly. I will reach out to my second-in-command to see if anyone has been injured or killed."

"I say we hit the street and see what Sylvia has found out for us," Kyle said.

Aleksei loosened his fists. "Father and I will start reading Council law to see if there's a way for us to stop the vote if all else fails. Let's meet back here at ten a.m. tomorrow to discuss next steps."

Everyone stood, and Callie excused herself, saying she needed to take care of the boys. She walked out of the community center and down the street, her steps quickening until she practically ran to her house.

She slowed down when she got to the sidewalk in front of her home, for fear that Irina would be looking out the window. Callie walked into the house and found Irina sitting at the kitchen table with a cup of coffee.

"Are the boys okay?" Callie asked.

"They're fine. They both went to bed with no fuss." Irina stood and took her coffee mug to the sink. "I take it from the look on your face the Council call didn't go well."

"The Council is going to vote tomorrow night on whether or not they should stop the demon immigration."

"Close-minded idiots, every dang one of them. I would ask for more details, but you look tired."

"Thank you, Irina, for watching the boys, and for...everything."

"No thanks are needed, my dear. You're clan now."

Callie stopped herself from flinching at Irina's declaration. She walked Irina to the door, and when she opened it, Grigori was standing on the front stoop. She wasn't sure where he had been hiding.

Once Irina and her guard were gone, she hurried down the hall to her sons' room, opened the door, and checked on them. They were both sound asleep, and she watched them until tears threatened to fall. She closed their door and leaned up against it for a moment, closing her eyes. Taking several deep breaths, she attempted to calm her heart, even though she knew what it was telling her.

It's time to go.

It wasn't as if she hadn't done this before. She found the twins' backpacks and loaded them with their favorite toys and games. She had just done laundry, and luckily hadn't had a chance to put the clothes away. She ran into the laundry room and grabbed first one laundry basket, and then another, placing them on the couch. Next she went into her kitchen and filled up a couple of her cloth grocery bags with food to take with them on the road.

A knock at her door ramped her heart rate back up into overdrive. Who would be here now? She opened the door a crack and found Misha gazing down at her with concern.

"I'm sorry to be here so late, Callie, but I want to be sure you and the boys are okay."

Callie attempted to smile. "We're good. The boys are asleep, and I'm heading there soon myself."

"Good. I know it's been a rough day for them and for you. I…" He looked over her shoulder and frowned.

Damn. She had opened the door too far. He was staring at the bags in her living room.

"What are you doing, Callie?"

"I'm not doing anything," she answered sharply.

"It looks to me like your packing bags to leave. You have to stop running."

Needles pricked along her skin. "You don't get to tell me how to protect my sons."

"If I thought this was only about your sons, I would agree."

"What the hell is that supposed to mean?"

"It means that I think this is about you not trusting us to help you."

Callie shook her head. "You say that now, but what happens if the clan doesn't want to help us anymore?"

"The clan would never abandon you, Callie."

"They might not have a choice in the matter. If the Council votes to stop the realm demon immigration, the next step might be to send the realm demons who already live here back—*including my sons!*"

Misha grabbed her shoulders. "Callie! Listen to me. I will not let anyone take your sons. It won't come to that."

"I can't risk anything happening to them."

"And you think hiding away with your sons is the answer? Your boys will need help with their demon side as they get older. Don't run."

Callie glared at him. "That's a bit hypocritical coming from you, isn't it? You've been hiding the truth about your powers from your family for years. Don't stand there now and judge me."

Misha flinched, and she instantly regretted lashing out at him.

"You're right. I'm going to have to apologize to my family for that. It was wrong. Learn from my mistakes, don't follow them."

"Why do you care so much what happens to me and the boys?" she asked.

His eyes darkened and he stared at her hard before responding. "Because I do."

"I'm scared, Misha," she whispered.

He pulled her in for a hug, and it felt right. God, she was in love with him. But before she could settle into his embrace, he held her again at arm's length.

"We're all here for you, Callie. You and the boys. Stay. If the vote goes badly tomorrow, I will protect you. Even if that means finding a place where you can start over. Stay for now, yes?"

Callie nodded. She would stay for now. But her boys were her first priority. She would leave everything behind, including the male she had fallen in love with, in order to protect them.

CHAPTER 24

Misha paced the BSR office. The Council meeting was tonight, and they had nothing concrete to tell them. Naya had spoken to her second-in-command, and most of the guards were accounted for. However, several were on patrol and had not been back to the guard camp for a couple of days.

They were running out of time.

And instead of being his normal, problem-solving self, he couldn't get Callie out of his damn head. Their conversation kept repeating like a mantra in his brain.

Why do you care so much what happens to me and the boys?

Because I do.

And while that might have sounded like a cop-out answer, it wasn't. He did care. His gut churned at the idea of her leaving. Hell, every time he closed his eyes he saw her face, heard her laugh, and felt her against him again like when he held her last night.

Holy Fates! He was an idiot. Yes, he wanted to protect her, but he also wanted *her*. And it had taken her looking up at him with those gorgeous green eyes and telling him she was leaving for him to finally realize the truth.

They needed to convince the Council not to give in to their prejudice and to let the realm demons come to earth.

When Kyle walked in, he pounced on her. "Have we heard anything from Sylvia?"

"Yep," she said. "Sylvia should be here any minute. Said she has someone who can help us during the Council meeting today."

"We need all the help we can get," Misha grumbled.

Kyle frowned. "You okay, big guy?"

He could tell her part of the truth, right? "I'm worried about Callie. When I went to check on her last night, she was packing her bags and planned on running with the boys."

"Crap," Kyle said. "You can't really blame her for being scared."

"I don't. But I thought she was past this now. We're here to help her. Why won't she trust us?"

Kyle patted his arm. "Mish, she hasn't had anyone to help her in the past. Think about how long it took for me to trust you and Jean Luc. You have to be patient with her."

"I can't be patient with her if she's not here!"

Kyle's eyes widened at his rather loud response.

It was time to dial back his reactions. The last thing he needed was Kyle getting involved with his feelings for Callie. "Sorry, little one."

Luckily, before Kyle could give him a tongue-lashing, Sylvia walked into the office with a large male following close behind. She smiled at them both before gesturing to the male.

"Kyle and Misha, this is Galim. He's originally from the realm."

"Has he had contact with the guy in the picture?" Kyle asked.

"No," Sylvia said. "The guy in the picture has been telling anyone who will listen that the Council is going to stop the immigration."

"That's nothing new. We're meeting to discuss that tonight."

"No, you misunderstand. He's been telling them this for *weeks* now."

"Why?"

"If I had to guess," Sylvia said. "I'd say it's to get them fired up. We have demons here who communicate telepathically with demons in the realm. If they believe they have been lied to..."

"...they'll attack," Misha finished for her.

"And prove that it's not safe for the realm demons to come to earth."

Kyle slammed her fist into her palm. "Damn. They're using their fear against them."

"Now that we know, how are we going to prove it?" Misha asked.

"That's where Galim comes into play," Sylvia said.

"Do you have information for us, Galim?" Kyle asked.

"Not yet," he answered softly.

What does that mean?

Kyle was apparently at a loss as well, since she looked at Sylvia with raised eyebrows.

Sylvia smiled. "Galim is what I would call a demon realm divining rod. As you know, most realm demons can sense other realm demons here on earth. Galim's senses are even more fine-tuned. Show them what I mean."

Galim looked at Kyle for a moment. "You're part human, but also part realm demon as well." He concentrated for a moment. "You are also carrying something from the realm."

Kyle frowned for a moment. "No...Wait." She pulled the necklace with the realm crystal she used to communicate with Naya out from under her shirt. "That's a pretty nifty gift you have."

Galim bowed his head slightly.

Kyle hesitated for a moment before speaking again. "Can you tell me what clan I come from?"

"From what I can sense, I think you're Majock."

Kyle gasped, and Misha placed his hand on her shoulder.

"Thank you. I didn't think I would ever know."

Galim nodded before turning to Misha. "You are Shamat, correct?"

"Yes."

"I can sense the different clans on earth, but I am still learning how to associate the feelings with the particular clans here." His eyes narrowed on Misha. "You have been spending time near other realm demons as well." He paused. "I want to say two demons, but they feel the same."

"Twins. Can you tell what clan they're from?"

Galim shook his head. "I would need to be near them to do that."

Kyle's eyes widened. "We've got to introduce him to the boys."

He nodded, although they didn't have time now. But as soon as the Council meeting was over, they would see if Galim could identify the boys' clan.

"Thank you for helping us, Galim," Misha said.

"I want my fellow demons to be able to come to earth."

Kyle smiled. "Well, your power could definitely come in handy during this meeting."

"Exactly," Sylvia said. "If anyone at the meeting has been spending time with realm demons, Galim can alert us."

Misha blew out a hard breath. Were they finally getting a break? Could they determine who was spreading lies among the realm demons to incite a war? And if they could stop this, could he then convince

Callie to stay? Because when this was all over, he would be discussing a few things with Callie Roberts.

———————————

The Council leaders were arriving at the community center with their entourages in tow. Misha had to work hard not to roll his eyes at the posturing that had already begun.

Misha stood next to Jean Luc at the front of the meeting hall, watching the space fill up. Boris greeted everyone with his usual panache, but Misha knew that behind his father's showiness was a brilliant mind. Every comment or gesture he made was for a purpose. Which was another reason why Misha would not be a good clan leader.

His brother was not as smooth as their father, but he was decisive and logical, again something the clan needed. Prior to the arrivals, Misha and Kyle had introduced Aleksei and Naya to Galim, so that they knew why he was in the room.

Josiah Akers, the Pavel leader, walked in with three aides, followed by the Haltrap leader with two huge males who were obviously bodyguards.

Kyle walked over and stood beside them. "Here I thought we might luck out and be able to recognize the bearded guy from the picture. Have you noticed how many males are sporting facial hair? Is this the new trend? I must have missed the newest edition of *Demon Quarterly.*"

Misha covered his mouth to hide his chuckle. "Clever, little one. I'm not sure what has inspired the goatee frenzy we're seeing today."

"Hopefully Galim will be able to help," Kyle said.

They watched Galim as he stood by the main entrance, concentrating on each demon as they entered the room. Kyle waved to Sylvia, and the small woman hustled over to join them.

"Has he gotten any hits yet?" Kyle asked.

"He's not a drug-sniffing dog, Kyle. He'll let us know if he senses something."

The last of the Council leaders entered the room, and Boris shepherded them to their seats around the large conference table at the front of the space, while their aides, bodyguards, and other hangers-on took seats in the audience section of the room.

Naya, who had been walking around the room in her demon form, now stood at the back by the entrance, looking fierce in her armor. No one would get by her if they tried to escape.

Galim wound his way to them through the audience chairs.

"Well?" Kyle asked impatiently.

"I can sense realm demon. The female with the red dress in the middle of the table has been around several realm demons."

Misha was surprised. "She is the Dalmot Council leader, Amelia Watkins. Who else?" he asked.

"One of the two males on the end has been around realm demons, but their guards won't let me get close enough to determine which one it is."

Galim gestured toward the Valtram leader, Peter Solomon, and Josiah Akers, the Pavel leader.

"Solomon had been one of the more vocal opponents of the immigration," Misha said.

"I hope it's Akers. I want to pin that bastard for something," Kyle growled.

Misha agreed. Akers had been a suspect in a previous case, and the team had never been able to prove he was guilty, even though Kyle was convinced of it.

"I am not sure," Galim said.

"Wishful thinking." Kyle clenched her fists, and Misha braced himself to grab her around the waist to stop her before she attacked the Pavel.

"It's time to call the meeting to order," Boris announced.

Kyle walked to the table and took her seat. As the spokesperson for the immigration project, she would not be left out of tonight's discussion.

Boris spoke for a few moments, opening the meeting before turning to the subject they were all waiting to discuss.

"Before we vote, the BSR team would like to report on the recent attack. Kyle."

Kyle nodded. "Our investigation has turned up some interesting information. For weeks now, rumors have been spread to the realm demon population that we plan to discontinue the immigration plan. And the rumors have been coming from demons on earth."

"For what purpose?" the Haltrap leader asked.

"To incite panic. To anger the realm demons into attacking us."

"Which they have done. Which proves they can't be trusted," Solomon replied.

"I tend to agree," Akers said.

Kyle tensed and leaned forward, warning Misha that she was about ready to explode into action. He placed his hand on her arm.

"I have a question for all of you," Kyle said, looking around the table at the Council leaders. "Have any of you actually spent any time talking with those you want to condemn to the realm?"

"I have," Council Leader Watkins said. "Today I spoke to some of the demons who arrived in the first immigration. I wanted to understand what their world was like before coming to earth."

"And what did you learn?" Aleksei asked.

"That they have been living in hell, and they want to have a chance at a life here on earth."

"Did they strike you as uncontrollable animals?" Kyle pressed.

"No."

"Anyone else?" Kyle asked. "Council Leader Solomon?"

"No. I do not trust them. We have a delicate balance of power on earth. We don't need to add more volatility here."

"You seem to be the only volatile one here right now," Kyle said.

Solomon glanced at his aide, who stood at the back of the room and—what do you know?—he had a beard. The aide shook his head slightly.

Misha sat up straighter and glanced at Jean Luc, who took a step closer to the aide from his spot along the wall.

Boris spoke up. "I think it is premature to cast our vote now. There is obviously something going on that we need to research further."

"I agree," Council Watkins said.

Solomon slammed his fists on the table. "No! It's time to stop this."

"What are you so scared of?" Kyle asked.

"These demons are monsters. My father told me how they destroyed our village. He was one of the few who survived. He moved with the survivors to a sister clan, and they were adopted in, but were never treated the way they were in their own clan. Do you know what it took for me to rise up to be the leader of my clan? I will not allow these animals to come back to earth to destroy us again."

"What have you done?" Boris demanded.

Solomon jerked to his feet. "What the rest of you should have done but were too scared to do! Stop those monsters from coming to earth!"

"You convinced them to attack yesterday," Boris said as he stood.

The other council leaders leapt to their feet as well.

Solomon ran around the table, aiming for Irina's chair in the audience as if he was going to grab her. Irina flicked her wrist, throwing him against the wall like a rag doll.

Red blurred Misha's vision as he shoved through the Council leaders to confront Solomon. "You threaten my babushka?"

The Council leader struggled to get to his feet. Misha jerked him up and slammed him against the wall. A scuffle sounded to the side of him. Out of the corner of his eye he could see Naya slam Solomon's aide to the ground.

Galim walked over to Misha. "He is carrying something from the realm."

Misha searched Solomon's coat and pulled out a silver cylinder from his breast pocket. "This is a portal device like the guards use. You are planning *another* attack!"

Everyone started talking at once.

"Quiet!" Aleksei shouted. "When are they attacking?"

"He should have already attacked. The bastard owes me, and he betrayed me."

Misha frowned. "Why do you say he owes you? What did you promise him?"

Solomon sealed his lips and shook his head.

Misha pressed his forearm to his chest. "Tell me, or I'll send you to the realm myself!"

"He asked me about the human woman and her half-demon brats. I told him he could have them if he attacked."

Misha handed Solomon over to Aleksei, his nerves sizzling under his skin. "I have a bad feeling. We need to get—"

Galim called out. "A portal just opened up somewhere in the compound."

"Callie!" Misha bellowed as he ran toward the door, Jean Luc and Kyle right behind him.

CHAPTER 25

Callie had been stress-baking, and now stood in the middle of her messy kitchen, mixing bowls, measuring spoons, rolling pin, and cookie racks littering her counter. Open flour and sugar bags sat nearby. The boys had begged her for cookies, which she gladly agreed to so she could get her mind off of the upcoming Council meeting.

Naturally the boys were already out on the jungle gym. Eating cookies was far more fun for seven-year-old boys than measuring, mixing, rolling, cutting and baking.

She looked around the room and sighed. It wasn't going to clean itself, and it was either keep busy or obsess about the Council vote, that…she looked at her clock…should be happening now. Although Kyle had warned her that it could be hours before she heard anything.

The front door opened. Someone was here already? Her stomach jumped. It couldn't be good news if it was over so soon.

"Is the vote over alread—" The cookie sheet she held clattered to the floor.

The scar-faced orange demon stood in her kitchen doorway.

She bit back a scream. She didn't want the boys to hear her and come back into the house.

Naya had told her about the different realm demon clans. "You're Kelmar."

The demon in front of her changed to human and she scrambled back.

But he's dead…isn't he?

"Mark?"

He scowled. "No. Markel is dead. He was my twin brother."

Twin? "I don't understand."

"Of course you don't. I told Markel we shouldn't come to earth, but he insisted. Since we were dying out in the realm, he wanted to prove that we could continue our clan here. And then he was killed by some demon who sensed that he was not from here. Such a waste, especially since I thought he'd been killed before he was able to father any children."

He grimaced. "I never understood what he saw in you. We were both at the bar the night he decided to approach you. After that I stayed away, but I watched him seduce you. You were so gullible, really."

Callie backed up until she bumped against the counter.

"When I came through the portal and saw you, I knew you must have had his children. Why else would a human woman be allowed to live in a demon compound? And when I was told you had twins, I knew it was true. Where are the boys? They're coming with me."

"No! I won't let you take them."

He laughed. "Do you honestly think you have a say in the matter? This planet is full of spoiled weaklings. I told Mark that he should have beaten you into submission back then, but he insisted on doing it his way."

"I won't let you harm my sons." Rage bubbled from her stomach into her throat. "No one will control me again."

The demon barked out a harsh laugh. "Hypocrite. Pretty strong words from someone who is being kept by the clan leader's son."

Callie frowned. "I don't know what you're talking about."

His eyebrows rose as he took a step toward her. "You live in his house. He has brought you into his clan. Are you not spreading your legs in payment to him?"

"No!" Callie yelled.

The patio door opened and the boys ran inside, stopping at the sight of the demon.

She rushed to put herself between the demon and her sons, but the demon grabbed her arm. Callie cried out when his claws punctured her arm.

"Run boys! Find Misha, go!"

But the boys stood frozen.

"Stay where you are," the demon growled. "You don't want anything to happen to your mother, do you?"

They both shook their heads.

"Good. If you come with me, I'll let your mother go."

"No! Run!" But the boys stood side by side in the door. Callie bit back a sob as she looked around, praying to find some sort of weapon.

The demon turned her to face him, his face contorting into a hideous smile. "Seems your sons might be smarter than you are."

Out of the corner of her eye, Callie saw the bag of flour sitting on the counter move slightly, but she didn't dare look over at Luke for fear the demon would sense something was going on. The bag rattled as it lifted into the air.

The demon turned when he heard the noise, and Callie ducked as the bag exploded, shooting flour into his face.

He coughed and sputtered, letting her go so he could wipe his eyes.

"Run, boys!"

They ran out the back door.

Callie grabbed the large wooden rolling pin off the counter and swung it like a baseball bat, connecting it with the side of the demon's head. He staggered, and she kicked him in the groin—hard.

When he bent forward clutching himself, she let fly with the rolling pin again. The front door slammed open, and Misha and Jean Luc ran into the room in time to see the pin crash against the demon's jaw.

The demon dropped to his knees, and before Callie could land another blow, Jean Luc disappeared and then reappeared behind the demon, cuffing him and shoving him to the ground.

A deep, familiar voice spoke next to her ear, and she jumped. She looked up into beautiful blue eyes. Eyes that checked her over with concern.

"Are you okay? Your arm is bleeding."

"I'm fine. Where are the boys?"

"They're safe out front with Kyle. We were coming down the walk when they ran around the side of the house."

She nodded as she watched Jean Luc drag away the demon.

"He's Mark's twin. He was going to take the boys." She blinked back tears.

"Callie, you can let go of the rolling pin."

She still gripped the pin like it was a lifeline. He held out his hand, and she willed her fingers to loosen. After a few moments, it fell into his hand.

"Momma!"

She spun toward the voices as her sons dashed into the room, and she dropped to her knees to hug them.

"Watch her arm, boys."

Matty's eyes widened when he caught sight of her arm. Luke squirmed out of Callie's grip, grabbed a kitchen towel, and placed it gently on the wound. Her heart swelled at how grown-up they were getting.

"You were so brave," Callie said. "Blowing up that flour in his face was very smart thinking."

The boys' chests puffed up.

Misha smiled down at the boys. "Your mom needs to go to the infirmary to have her arm checked out."

"I'm not leaving the boys—" Callie announced.

"We're not leaving Momma—" the boys announced at the same time.

"I wouldn't think of it. We're going to the infirmary together."

A few minutes later, Callie sat on a gurney while Doctor Miller cleaned her arm. She took some deep breaths to get her heart rate to calm.

"Are you okay?" Sabrina asked as she gave Callie an injection to numb the area she was going to stitch up.

Callie looked out the small window in the exam room door and saw the boys sitting with Kyle in the hall. "I'm fine."

Sabrina didn't look like she believed Callie, but she finished up in a few minutes and left her to prepare an antibiotic injection for her as an added precaution.

The door opened and Misha stepped inside. "I'm so glad you're okay."

Callie nodded.

"I wanted to let you know it's over, Callie. We caught the people behind the protests and attacks, and the Council has voted to continue the immigration."

She blew out a breath and blinked back tears as she looked through the window at her sons. They were talking to a tall man.

"Who is that?" Callie asked.

"Galim. He's a realm demon who helped us earlier. He alerted us when the portal opened so we could get to you and Matty and Luke. Of course we didn't know at the time that you had already taken care of the demon yourself. I wanted him to meet the boys to confirm that they're Kelmar."

"Can I talk to him?" Callie asked.

"Of course." Misha opened the door and beckoned to Galim, who entered the room with Sabrina.

Callie waited until the door was closed before speaking. "Thank you for letting the team know we were being attacked."

Galim smiled. "It was my honor. Your boys are special."

"They're Kelmar?"

"Yes."

"Naya told me about the realm demon clans. She said that Kelmar manipulate energy and space."

"Yes," Galim said. "Twins born to the clan are often Abstatholm.

Callie's heart pounded. "The twins can create portals?"

"Possibly. That is not something I can discern." He studied her for a moment, as if she was a puzzle he couldn't figure out.

"What is it, Galim?" Misha asked.

He kept staring at Callie. "I sense something different about you. You are not realm demon, but you have realm inside you."

"I don't understand."

Misha stepped closer to her. "What do you think, Sabrina?"

"I can run some tests, but I'm not sure if I'll find anything definitive. Callie gave birth to twins. We have little information so far regarding how a human female's body changes when having a realm demon child."

Galim nodded. "Yes. I do sense your sons' energy inside you."

Sabrina shooed Misha and Galim out of the room so she could give Callie the shot and wrapped her arm in gauze.

Sabrina gave her a quick once-over. "You sure you're okay?"

"I'm fine." But was she really? Because now she and the boys were out of danger, she was stewing about what the Kelmar demon had said to her about being a kept woman.

Was the house Misha's, and had everyone been lying to her all along?

She had told Mark's brother that she would never let anyone control her again, and she meant that from the bottom of her soul.

When Sabrina walked out, Misha stepped back inside.

"Let's get you home. You and the boys are safe now."

Callie closed her eyes. Her boys were safe. That was what mattered.

But she needed to be safe too.

"Callie, are you sure you're okay? Do you want me to go get Sabrina?"

She opened her eyes and looked at him. "Misha, the demon who attacked me tonight said we are living in your house. Why would he say that?"

Now was when he was going to tell her the demon was wrong.

He hesitated, and she filled in the gaps, anger fueling her words.

"You lied to me. This has all been a fantasy."

"The house is mine. I'm sorry, Callie. I should've told you the truth."

"Yes, you should have." She stood. "Do you know how long I have worked to take care of myself and my boys? Me. No one else. Because anyone I have ever let close to me betrays me, manipulates me, controls me. And I told you that. I shared my past with you, and you still *lied* to me. How could you do that?"

"I…"

"How!"

"I wanted to protect you and the boys."

Like they were a charity. "It doesn't justify what you did."

"I knew you wouldn't move here if I told you the truth."

"You convinced everyone to lie to me! The whole clan must feel sorry for me." She paced in the small room. None of it made sense. "Why do you have that monstrosity of a swing set in your backyard?"

"I had it installed before I showed you the house. Let me explain. I need to tell you someth—"

"Stop!" She jerked to a halt. "I can't do this anymore, Misha."

"Do what?"

"Stay here. It's time for the boys and me to move."

"Callie, please don't go. You don't have to run anymore."

"I'm not running, Misha. I won't sneak out in the night like I've done in the past. I'll find a job and a clan where the boys can learn what it means to be demon."

He frowned. "You can do that here. I won't bother you anymore."

She shook her head. "I can't. I need to start over and prove to my boys that I can provide what they need."

He claimed everything he did was to keep them safe. Not because he had feelings for her, but because he felt sorry for her. But what he didn't understand was that she wasn't safe from him. Her heart, especially.

In the past Callie didn't believe she deserved someone to love her.

Now she knew better.

It was time for her to build a life she and her sons could be proud of. And if she didn't get away from the male standing in front of her, the one who owned her heart, she would never be able to find someone else to possibly give it to someday.

───────────

Callie sat on the back patio watching the boys as they raced around the yard, squealing as the sprinklers soaked them. It wouldn't be too long before the days would grow colder. Plus she wasn't sure whether the boys would have a yard where they were moving next.

"Hello?"

"Back here," she called out.

Sabrina walked around the side of the house carrying a small black bag. She waved to the boys before she sat down with Callie at the patio table.

"Making a house call, Doc?"

"Yep." She opened her bag. "Let's take a look at your arm." Sabrina unwrapped it and inspected it closely. "Well, I'll be."

"What's wrong?" Callie asked.

"Nothing. You're almost healed, which is what I would expect from a demon, not a human."

Callie looked down at her arm. "How?"

"I think it has to do with what Galim said the other day. Let me ask you something. Do you get sick often?"

Callie thought about it for a moment before responding. "No. I don't remember the last time I was sick. Maybe before the twins were born."

Sabrina smiled. "I think the boys left you a gift. They spent nine months in you, and gave you some of their healing ability."

"Wow."

"That's what I think too. I'm not sure how else your DNA has been impacted. With enhanced healing often comes a prolonged life. But I don't want us to count our chickens before they hatch. I'd like to test some of your blood and see what it tells me."

Sabrina left a few minutes later with a vial of blood after promising to get back to Callie. She sat back. Maybe she would get to spend more time on earth with her boys.

Before she could call for the boys to come inside, Kyle walked around to the back of the house.

"Kyle!" The boys yelled before running full tilt toward her and slamming their wet bodies against her.

"Boys!" Callie admonished.

Kyle laughed. "You little demons! I'll get you for that." She grabbed the hose, pressing the nozzle and spraying them both.

Ten minutes later, Callie herded the boys into the house for a shower. She brought a towel out to a dripping Kyle on the patio.

"Man, that was fun," Kyle said, scrubbing her hair with the towel. "The boys seem to be doing pretty well since the other night."

"They're good. It's amazing to me how resilient children can be."

"And what about you? Are you going to be able to bounce back from this?"

"I'll get there eventually."

Kyle sat down at the patio table, and Callie joined her.

"You've been through a lot this past year, Callie."

Callie ran her hands over the frosted glass tabletop. "That might be the understatement of the year."

Kyle chuckled before turning serious. "I'm sorry for everything that's happened to you."

Callie shrugged. "You had no control over Mark Stewart, or his deranged brother, any more than you had over your own parentage."

"True. But I know you're just as upset about the house, maybe more. I don't have the right, but I'm going to ask you anyway. Please don't hate Misha."

Callie sighed. "I could never hate him. But what he did was wrong."

"If you're going to blame him, you need to blame the rest of us as well. We went along with his crazy idea."

"I told Misha what happened to me in my childhood, and what I endured with Mark. He knew that trust is the one thing I have trouble giving. That I need to have a hand in controlling my future and the future of my sons. But he still lied to me. He brought me into this clan and attempted to plan my life out for me. Getting me a job, moving me into his house. He created a fantasy world that can't last forever.

"I can't let my boys get attached and then be disappointed when everything they thought was real falls apart around them."

"I can tell you in Misha's defense that he wasn't trying to create a fantasy for you, but a reality."

Callie gazed out at the empty play set and didn't speak for a moment. "I'm sure Misha told you already, but I've decided to leave. And before you say it, I'm not running away. I'm moving forward. Aleksei put out some feelers for me, and there is a Dalmot clan in Atlanta looking for an office manager for their paper supply business. The boys and I are going to move there. Get a fresh start. The clan leader knows about Matty and Luke and is willing to help them with their powers as they progress. I'll never be able to repay you and the clan for what you've done for me, but I need to stand on my own."

Kyle didn't respond for several minutes. Finally, she spoke. "I don't know if you've heard this story or not, but Misha actually delivered me."

Callie swiveled in her chair and faced Kyle.

"My mother was attacked by a demon when she was nine months pregnant. A demon who was actually trying to stop me from being born. Luckily Jean Luc, Talia, and Misha were able to stop him. Misha didn't know my mother, but he didn't want her to be alone. So he took her to the hospital to be checked out, and when they were both trapped in an elevator, Misha delivered me. And Misha being Misha, when he found out my mother was an unwed teenage mother whose family kicked her out, he wanted to help us both.

"After I was born, someone came to the hospital and warned my mother that more demons would come after her and me if she didn't hide. So she ran off and changed our names. Sounds familiar huh?"

Callie nodded.

"Misha didn't know anything about this. He only knew that my mom had left the hospital with me, and back then he didn't know how to find us."

Kyle cleared her throat. "Unlike you, my mother made it very clear as I was growing up that she blamed me for her less-than-stellar life. When I turned nineteen I was recruited to work for the BSR, and I met Misha for what I thought was the first time. A year ago we both discovered that he's the one who brought me into this world. And when he found out what my childhood was like, it almost crushed him. He still blames himself for not helping me. Misha carries the weight of the world on his shoulders and the caring for everyone he meets in his heart. He can't help but help."

Callie closed her eyes. "Kyle, I don't know what to say. But I can't afford to let someone close to me like that...to take over my life the way he did."

"I get what you're saying. More than you will ever know. Or at least the old Kyle got it. I used to be so scared of letting anyone near me that I built this foot-thick wall of defensiveness around me to keep everyone away. I thought it was so much easier to not rely on anyone. Because then they couldn't let me down."

Kyle rested her hand over Callie's, and Callie opened her eyes. "Here's the thing. Misha and Jean Luc chiseled away on that wall I had around me until I couldn't help but let them in. If I hadn't done that, I would have missed out on the life I have now, and I would have never let Dalton near my heart.

"You say you can't afford to allow anyone to get close, but I would argue that you can't afford *not* to."

CHAPTER 26

The last thing Misha wanted to do right now was attend a family dinner. He had to figure out how to win Callie back. Hell, who was he kidding? He needed to *win* her. He hadn't had her to begin with.

But Babushka had insisted on the dinner, and it was very hard to say no to Babushka. Kyle was there since, like it or not, she had become a member of his family when he proclaimed her to be his *sestra*.

But for some reason Jason, Sabrina, Talia, and Jean Luc were there as well. Which was a little strange since Talia and Jean Luc weren't going to be eating. Even Joe had been invited and was sitting next to Kyle. And they were still pretty clingy even though Joe had been home for a few days now. Misha had worried for a long time that Kyle wouldn't be able to open her heart to someone. Ironic, really, considering his own situation.

So Misha sat at the table with Aleksei and Boris talking at one end, and Kyle and Irina talking at the other, and the rest of the team gabbing in the middle. Misha had nothing to say while he pushed the food around on his plate.

"Is something wrong with the food?" Irina asked.

"No. I'm just not hungry."

All talking stopped, and he looked up from his plate to find everyone at the table staring at him.

Irina frowned. "Are you sick?"

"No."

"Then tell me what's wrong. You not eating is like the rest of us not breathing."

Misha set down his fork. "I can't stop thinking about Callie and the boys. I don't want them to go."

"None of us want to see them go. But it's Callie's decision. I know how much you have become attached to Matty and Luke."

And damn, Misha did care for those boys. They had become a part of his heart. But right now the green eyes he pictured belonged to their pretty mother. Should he tell his interfering family and friends the truth?

"I don't want Callie to go."

"Why?" Irina asked.

Misha hesitated. There were so many reasons. He couldn't get her out of his head. She challenged him, and he wanted to be a part of her life as well as the boys' lives. Did that mean—wait. His heart tripped, and his chest burned like it did after eating atomic wings on twenty-five cent wing night. He *loved* her.

Jean Luc blurted. "Because you love her, *espèce d'idiot!*"

Misha gaped at his seldom-ruffled teammate. Jean Luc's face was actually red.

Talia grabbed her vampire mate's hand as if to calm him and then huffed at Misha. "You *are* being an idiot, you know."

Jason and Sabrina nodded as well.

Misha didn't dare look at Kyle to see her reaction.

"Fine, I'm an idiot. And you're right. I do love her."

Irina and Kyle gave each other a high five as the rest of the table cheered.

"It's about damn time, grandson. I never thought you would get there," Irina announced.

Aleksei slapped his hand to the table. "I knew you loved her when you kept threatening me if I so much as looked at her, or touched her, or breathed around her."

Boris beamed. "He is quite smitten with her."

Talia chuckled. "You should have seen how he—"

"Enough!" Misha threw his hands in the air. "Why didn't any of you say anything?"

He glared at the group before settling his ire on his grandmother and Kyle. "And if you all are so brilliant, why in the world would you push me towards Naya?"

Irina sighed. "Don't blame Kyle for trying to get you to spend time with Naya. I convinced her to do this my way." Irina stood from her place at the head of the table and walked over to him. He stood as well, and she placed her hand on the middle of his chest. "You are an amazing male. You are honest…for the most part—don't think I won't be talking to you later about you hiding your powers—you are loyal, and you have an enormous heart that insists on protecting everyone." Irina patted the place over his heart. "All of these traits are wonderful. But you are a train wreck when it comes to romantic relationships."

Jason nodded again.

"Stop it," Misha growled at his friend. "You look like a bobblehead doll."

He turned back to his grandmother. "How can you say I'm bad at relationships? If it wasn't for me, Talia and Jean Luc would never have gotten together. And I was the one who talked the team into helping me convince Kyle and Dalton they were being stupid and to give each other another chance."

"Hey!" Kyle sputtered.

"Not now, dear," Irina said. "You and Dalton were being dumb."

Kyle crossed her arms and looked ready to spit nails.

Dalton wrapped his arm around her shoulder and kissed her head. "Shh. Now we're not the only dumb ones when it comes to love. Let Irina talk."

Irina's gaze zeroed in on Misha again.

Apparently, his babushka was not finished with him yet.

"Mikhail, you are a hopeless romantic. And while you have helped your friends find their true loves, you haven't been able to find your own. Love is not grand gestures and fairy tales. It is finding that one person you can't live without. That person who invades your thoughts at the most inopportune times.

"The day I met Callie I knew she was the one for you. But I didn't dare say anything, because you have never listened to my advice when it comes to your heart. If anything, you do the opposite. But what I did know is that you needed to get this romantic notion that Naya was your happy-ever-after out of your brain. A conclusion that you came to simply by looking at her. So I pushed you to at least talk to her. If you didn't, you would never have let the romantic notion die."

"I've spoken to her," Misha protested.

"Have you really talked to her? And I don't mean about the case. Have you spent time with her, learning about what she wants out of life?"

It didn't take long for Misha to think about his answer. "No."

"Exactly. Now tell me about Callie."

"Callie is stubborn and fearless when it comes to protecting her sons. She wants her sons to learn about what it means to be demon, and what it means to be part of a real family. She wants a job where she feels she is contributing something important. And she doesn't want to have to rely on others to help her. Which is silly. Everyone needs someone to rely on."

"And you're her someone, grandson. So what are you going to do to fix this?"

"I've been trying to figure that out since I realized I loved her."

"In the last three minutes?" Kyle said.

"No. I had already figured it out before my teammate called me an idiot."

Irina smiled. "So you didn't need us to tell you so?"

"No." Misha's gaze dropped to the ground. "But I don't know whether she'll be willing to listen to me. To forgive me."

Babushka's fingers touched his chin, and he raised his face to look at her.

"Since when has that ever stopped you before?"

"Yep, big guy," Kyle said. "Have you wondered why she can forgive the rest of us for lying to her, but not you? She's so upset because she has feelings for you."

Could that be true?

"Yeah," Aleksei said. "You need to fix this so I don't lose the best office manager I've ever had."

Misha glared at him. "She's the only office manager you've ever had."

"That doesn't mean she's not the best. Fix this, big brother, or I'll make you lead the clan."

Boris cleared his throat. "Um, boys, I'm still alive and kicking. Not something you need to worry about right now."

Kyle held up her hands. "Enough! Misha, do you want Callie, Matty, and Luke to leave?"

His stomach dropped. "Of course not!"

"Then you better do something. Callie and the boys are leaving soon. She invited all of us over for lunch tomorrow."

"She didn't invite me."

"Actually, she did. I was supposed to tell you to come to say goodbye to the boys."

His chest tightened. "I will figure out how to stop this stubborn woman from leaving."

He would convince her to forgive him. Could she truly have feelings for him, as Kyle said? When the silence continued, he glanced around the table to see everyone looking extremely pleased with themselves.

Misha glared at them all. "This was not a family dinner."

"Nope," Kyle said. "We just did an intervention on your ass. Although it was a bit anticlimactic, since you already figured out you love Callie. But you should still thank us."

"Thank you."

Kyle nodded. "Now don't screw this up, big guy."

"*Oui, mon ami*," Jean Luc said. "Do not screw this up."

CHAPTER 27

Misha took a deep breath as he stood on Callie's front porch. Which he guessed would be his front porch soon enough if he couldn't convince her to stay. The butterflies fluttering around his stomach all morning had now morphed into pterodactyls attempting to explode out of his chest.

As he raised his hand to knock, he heard laughter coming from around the side of the house. He walked across the yard and around to the back. The patio was full of people. Kyle, Jean Luc, Talia, Jason, Joe, and Sabrina were there, along with his babushka, father, and brother.

And in the center sat Callie and the twins. When he saw her, his heart squeezed like it was in a vise. Jean Luc was right. He was an idiot.

Could he get her to listen, to give him another chance?

Hell. He had been so clueless about his feelings when it came to her, maybe he didn't deserve a second chance. But then she looked up at him, and her gorgeous green eyes were missing their sparkle.

That was unacceptable.

"Misha!" The boys hollered, running toward him and grabbing his legs. He hugged them both.

Irina clapped her hands together. "Well, now everyone's here, we can help get lunch ready."

When Callie stood, Irina held her hands up. "You relax. We'll take care of everything. I insist."

Irina directed the adults into the house like a drill sergeant, and then ushered the twins into the house as well.

"What was that about?" Callie asked.

"She wanted to give us some time alone. Babushka can never be called subtle."

Callie gazed at him in silence.

"I need to talk to you, Callie."

She sighed. "You don't have to apologize again, Misha. I understand that you feel this need to protect everybody. I appreciate what you did for the boys and for me. And like I told Kyle, I'm not running away, I'm finally going to move forward with my life."

"I think I'm the one who has been running, Callie."

She gave him a puzzled frown, but he continued. "I used to have this idea of what love is supposed to be. When I met Naya, I thought I had found what I was missing. But I fell in love with the idea of her. She was exotic and unattainable, which was perfect for me. But then you came along—the opposite of Naya."

Callie frowned harder. "Are you telling me I'm boring and attainable?"

Misha heard several groans and a French expletive in the house—stupid supernatural hearing. He didn't need an audience listening to him crash and burn.

He clenched his fists. *I am blowing it!*

He turned away from the house and beckoned for her to follow him over to the swing set and out of earshot from their audience. He couldn't afford to be distracted right now.

"I'm not saying this the right way. You are a wonderful, beautiful, smart woman, with the heart of a warrior, and I love you, Callie Roberts."

She blinked up at him.

"I am a stupid horse's ass for taking so long to figure it out, but I love you. I'm sorry I didn't see what was right in front of me. That's not true. I saw it, only I was too chicken to act on it. I have never done well with love. I thought I knew what love was, but I was woefully wrong.

"My grandmother told me last night that love isn't a fairy tale, but I think there is magic to it. I've been working so hard to find people to love for my family and friends because I was scared to try again for myself. But then I met you, and I can't get you out of my mind. I suppressed my feelings, insisting that everything I did was to protect you and the boys. And that was part of it, but the three of you have found your way into my heart. And I don't want you to go."

He swallowed. "I know I screwed up, and I'm sorry. I understand if you can't give me a second chance. I want to show you who I really am, so maybe someday you can find it in your heart to love me back."

He looked down at her. She was studying his face closely.

"Did you practice that speech?" she asked.

"No. But it came from my heart."

When she didn't say anything, he couldn't stand the silence anymore.

"It was a good speech, yes?"

His heart stopped when she turned from him without answering. She took a step away from him, and he cursed his stupidity, cursed his unwillingness to take a chance, cursed the Fates for waiting too long to tell this spitfire that she was the one for him.

"Don't leave," he said as he stepped toward her.

"Hush."

His mouth snapped shut at her one word. She stepped up onto the bottom of the slide so she was off the ground and could look him in the eyes...somewhat...and then cupped his face in her hands.

She stared at him for a long moment, and his frozen heart dared to beat one single time.

Thump.

"Yes, it was a very good speech. I like when you practice, but I really like it when you ad lib. It did take you a long time to get with the program, Misha Sokolov."

Thump, thump.

He opened his mouth, but she shook her head.

"I'm not finished yet. I see that I'm going to have to be a bit more straightforward with you in the future."

She stood on her tiptoes and rested her forehead against his.

Thump, thump, thump.

"I won't be able to find it in my heart to love you someday, Misha, because I love you now. I have for a while. At first, I didn't want to fall in love with you. In the past, I haven't been able to rely on anyone, but you showed me, over and over again, that I could turn to you." She backed away so he could look into her green eyes. "And you didn't have an agenda. You weren't expecting anything from me. Because you have an incredibly big heart. A heart that took a while to figure out what it needed, I might add, but it allowed this closed-off woman to risk opening herself to love."

There was no controlling his incredibly big heart now. Thumps turned into a rat-a-tat-tat high-speed pattern.

He rested his hands on her waist and leaned closer, and she placed her fingers over his lips, stopping his descent.

"They are all shamelessly watching us through the windows, aren't they?"

Callie laughed. "See for yourself."

Misha glanced back over his shoulder. Boris, Aleksei, and Irina watched through the kitchen window. Kyle, Jean Luc, Talia, Dalton, Sabrina, and Jason were crowded against the French doors. The twins stood in front of the team with their hands and faces pressed against the glass.

Misha's tipped his head back and laughed a deep belly laugh.

He looked down at her. "You do understand that if you stay with me, you're going to have to deal with my friends and family. We will never be truly alone."

Callie beamed up at him. "Except for my boys, I have been alone my whole life. You may think your family and friends are interfering, but I think you are a very lucky male. I would be blessed to have them in my life."

"Prepare yourself for sainthood, Callie. You will be blessed many times over, my love."

He released her for a moment and held two thumbs up toward the house. Everyone started to cheer and dance around.

But Misha turned away from them. He had more important matters to attend to.

He leaned down, capturing Callie's lips, and everything around them fell away. Her flavor was addictive. She was an amazing appetizer, an exceptional entrée, and a decadent dessert, all rolled into one.

And if he had his way, he'd never get his fill.

CHAPTER 28

Two Months Later

Callie reached for her glass when Boris proposed another toast. "Thank you for all your hard work in making the latest immigration a success."

Everyone at the long table raised their glasses and then took a sip. It had been a crazy week with the third group of realm demons arriving on earth. Callie had been working nonstop, and had barely seen Misha except in passing.

Misha wrapped his arm around Callie's shoulder and she leaned into him. "Your babushka has agreed to babysit the twins tonight."

Misha scooped a spoonful of potatoes with his other hand and placed it on his plate. "That was nice of her to offer. What would you like to do tonight? Go see a movie?"

She leaned closer to him and whispered. "I want you to make love to me."

He gaped at her. "What did you say?"

She brushed her lips against his ear. "I said, I want you to make love to me. I haven't been with anyone since before the twins were born. I love you, and I want to climb you like a big ol' tree."

The serving spoon Misha held fell from his hand, clattering against his plate. Everyone turned toward them.

Irina's eyes danced. "Is everything okay, Mikhail?"

"Yes. Um...I'm not that hungry."

Silence.

Callie managed not to laugh when Misha's face turned maroon.

"If you keep losing your appetite, you might want to have the doctor check you over, brother," Aleksei said with a ridiculous grin on his face.

"I th-think we're going to c-call it a night," Misha stammered.

"Of course, dear. It's been a long day for everyone," Irina said.

God bless Irina, she didn't torture her grandson... unlike his evil brother.

Misha stood and reached for Callie's chair.

"Aren't you going to stay for dessert?" Luke asked.

"I've got some dessert at the house," Callie said at the same time Kyle choked on a sip of water. Kyle spent a moment coughing, or was she laughing?

Callie ignored her friend. "You boys be good for Miss Irina tonight," Callie said.

"Yes, Momma," they chorused.

Before she could say any more goodbyes, Misha was pulling her along the back of the house toward the sidewalk.

"I can't believe you just told everyone you're not hungry."

"It only happens around you. My family will have to get used to it. Besides, how can you think about food at a time like this?"

"I was starting to think you didn't want me."

Misha jerked to a halt and spun to face her. "How can you think that? I have wanted to make love to you since the day you kissed me standing on that slide in your backyard. With everything that's been going on with the immigrations, our crazy schedule, and the boys, I could never find the right time to be alone with you."

"Which is why I took matters into my own hands."

Misha grabbed her hand. "Yes, you did. I love how resourceful you are."

They set a speed-walking record getting back to the house. Misha open the door, and before it clicked shut behind them, he had her in his arms.

He kissed her, his tongue delving inside her mouth to play, and hers joined in. She literally felt as if she was melting against him. He let her go for a moment and sucked in a large gulp of air, as if he hadn't been breathing while they were kissing. She understood the feeling.

She backed toward the bedroom, and his eyes took on a predatory glint. She giggled. *God, when was the last time she giggled?* She turned and ran toward the bedroom. He caught up with her in seconds, and she yelped when he flung her up over his shoulder.

When they made it to her bedroom, he laid her gently in the center of the bed, gazing down at her, his eyes raking her from head to toe. She was wearing jeans and a long sleeve T-shirt. She should've worn something sexier for tonight.

"You are so beautiful," he said in a gruff voice.

She held out her arms, and he crawled up the bed, caging her in with his body. She pulled his head down and kissed him, her tongue playing along his lower lip. He growled, and the sound ratcheted her heartbeat up until it pounded in her ears. He reached for her top at the same time she grabbed his shirt.

Moments later they were both skin to skin. And the feel of him had her purring. She wanted to rub against him like a contented cat.

Misha kissed her neck and then ran his tongue along her collarbone. Since when did touching her collarbone cause goosebumps? A whoosh of air escaped her, and Misha looked up at her.

His ice-blue eyes had darkened, and his grin warned her that he was about to be a very bad boy. He winked at her before moving down her body. And her gasps turned to moans while he got *very* creative. It had been so long since she had felt pleasure, but it had never been at nuclear meltdown levels before.

She shuddered, her vision going gray. She wasn't sure how much time had passed before she could see again. When she opened her eyes, Misha lay beside her.

"Are you ready for the second course?" he asked.

She reached for him. "Absolutely."

Lazy kisses turned hot and frenzied. He unwrapped a condom, slipped it on, and then he was finally inside her, shaking with the effort to go slowly.

"I won't break, Misha."

And then slow wasn't enough anymore and frenzied came back for a visit.

"I love you, Callie."

And as soon as he said it, Callie soared over the cliff, her body celebrating Valentine's Day, Fourth of July, and Mardi Gras all at once.

Misha brushed his lips over hers before lying next to her so he didn't crush her. He looked into her eyes while his fingers lightly stroked her face. "That was earth-shattering," he said.

Callie's heart tap-danced in her chest. "Yes, it was."

Misha's slumberous look changed to a cocky smirk. He continued to trace his fingers over her neck, moving it down to her collarbone.

"I was going to do this a different way. Plan a perfect evening, but I can't imagine anything more perfect than right now. I love you, Callie. Will you marry me?"

Callie's tap-dancing heart jerked to a stop, and she couldn't breathe, much less form words.

Misha looked at her expectantly, and she knew the old Callie would be running through all the reasons why she couldn't trust him or this to last. But she was the new Callie, the woman who didn't want to miss out on happiness and love because she was too afraid to trust another person with her heart.

"Yes. I'll marry you."

Misha let out a whoop and pulled her against him. This time when they made love it was slow and sweet.

When they were done, she laid her cheek on his chest. "So when do we tell everyone?"

Misha rested his chin against the top of her head. "Before we make it official, I have to do the proper thing and ask permission."

Callie snuggled against him. She still didn't understand everything about clan politics, but if he had to get permission from someone in the clan...his father or maybe the elders...in order to marry, she had no problem with that.

———————

Misha cleared his throat. It had been dry since the conversation started. "Do I have your permission to marry her?"

He looked over at the two males while he waited for an answer. They sat on the couch staring at him for a drawn-out moment. They looked over at Callie as well.

The twins then glanced at each other and seemed to communicate in their silent twin fashion.

The longer Misha waited for their response, the harder it was to swallow. It was only right to ask the boys for their mother's hand in marriage. After a few more throat-drying moments, the boys finally looked back at him.

Luke spoke. "You can marry Momma."

"But under one conviction," Matty added.

"It's called a condition," Callie said.

"What is your condition?" Misha asked.

Luke stared down at his feet. "We…um…want to know if we can call you Papa."

"It only makes sense, yes?" Matty said.

Misha blinked. Callie raised her hand to her mouth as tears glistened in her eyes. He cleared his throat again so he could choke the words out. "Yes, it makes perfect sense. I would be honored to be your papa."

The boys grinned.

He opened his arms and Matty and Luke jumped against him. Tears rolled down his cheeks as Callie wrapped her arms around her sons as well, and he kissed the boys' heads before leaning to capture her lips.

He had never tasted anything sweeter.

THANKS!

Thank you for taking the time to read Demons Will Be Demons. I hope you enjoyed Misha's happy ending and the first book in the Realm Series. Please consider telling your friends about it or posting a short review. Word of mouth is an author's best friend, and much appreciated. Thank you!

Demons Are A Girl's Best Friend, the next book in the series is going to focus on Aleksei. I think by now you probably have figured out who he is supposed to end up with...

If you would like to know when my next books will be released, please join my new releases email list at www.aejonesauthor.com or follow me on Twitter @aejonesauthor or Facebook at www.facebook.com/ aejones.author1

If you haven't had a chance to read my Mind Sweeper series that started this all, please see the series list on the next page.

Books by AE Jones

The Realm Series
(Mind Sweeper Spin Off)

Demons Will Be Demons
Demons Are A Girl's Best Friend
Demons Are Forever
Demons In The Rough
Demons Just Want To Have Fun

Mind Sweeper Series

Mind Sweeper – Book 1
The Fledgling – Book 2
Shifter Wars – Book 3
The Pursuit – Book 4
Sentinel Lost – Book 5

Mind Sweeper Flashback Story Bundle

Forget Me
Trust Me
Protect Me

Paranormal Wedding Planner Series

In Sickness and In Elf – Book 1
From This Fae Forward – Book 2
To Have and To Howl – Book 3
For Better or For Wolf – Book 4
For Witch or For Poorer – Book 5
Till Demon Do Us Part – Book 6

To find all of AE Jones's books, visit her website:
www.aejonesauthor.com

ABOUT THE AUTHOR

Growing up a TV junkie, AE Jones oftentimes rewrote endings of episodes in her head when she didn't like the outcome. She immersed herself in sci-fi and soap operas. But when *Buffy* hit the little screen, she knew her true love was paranormal. Now she spends her nights weaving stories about all variations of super-natural—their angst and their humor. After all, life is about both...whether you sport fangs or not.

AE won RWA's Golden Heart® Award for her paranormal manuscript, Mind Sweeper, which also was a RWA RITA® finalist for both First Book and Paranormal Romance. AE is also a recipient of the Booksellers' Best Award and is a National Readers' Choice Award Finalist, Holt Award of Merit Finalist and a Daphne du Maurier Finalist.

AE lives in Ohio surrounded by her eclectic family and friends who in no way resemble any characters in her books. *Honest.* Now her two cats are another story altogether.

Made in the USA
Middletown, DE
18 July 2021